CROMA, A WAY OF LIFE

D1637627

BY REGIS CASTRO

Raïssa – 2nd edition
Croma, a Way of Life
Pique
Barby
Rabboni – 2nd edition
The Endearing Hands of Mary – 2nd edition
Book of Divine Mercy – 2nd edition
Cod's Advice for You – 3rd edition

BY REGIS CASTRO AND MAÏSA CASTRO

Jesus Loves You – 3rd edition
Jesus Visits You (Rachel) – 2nd edition
Healing through Blessing (Blessing upon Blessing) – 2nd edition
Jesus Is My Friend – 2nd edition
The Powerful Hand of Jesus in My Heart – 2nd edition
Jesus Wants to Heal Your Life – 3rd edition
Book of the Family – Healing and Salvation for You and Your Family – 2nd edition
Ping-Pong Praise – 2nd edition
Rosary of Liberation – 7th edition
Eternal Love – 3rd edition
Testimonials about the Rosary of Liberation

BY MAÏSA CASTRO

You Must Be Born Again
Persevere in the Love of God – 3rd edition
God's Promises to You
Prayers of Power – 4th edition
Prayers of Power II – 2nd edition

Regis Castro

Croma
a Way of Life

Editors: Regis Castro/Maïsa Castro
Translation: Robert Hausemann
Revision: Gilbert R. Avelar
Cover: Estúdio Campos
Printed by: R. Vieira Gráfica e Editora Ltda. Campinas/SP

FOR THE GLORY OF JESUS CHRIST OUR LORD. ALLELUIA!

© 1991 by Raboni Editora Ltda.

All rights reserved. No part of this book may be reproduced or transmitted in any form or by any means, electronic or mechanical, including photo-copying, recording or by an information storage and retrieval system without the written permission of Raboni Editora Ltda.

ISBN 85-85592-36-2 (original edition)
ISBN 85-7345-109-2

Orders from:

• **RABONI EDITORA LTDA.**
  C. P. 1700 – CEP 13001-970 – Campinas/SP/Brasil
  PHONE NUMBER: 0055-19-3242-8433
  FAX: 0055-19-3242-8505

  Home page: http://www.raboni.com.br
  e-mail: raboni@raboni.com.br

To my beloved wife, *Maïsa,*
and all of mine.

Preface

The man and writer that I am today are a direct consequence of the companionship of the woman who has blessed my life. Together we have explored and experienced, during many nights and early morning hours, heated discussions about phrases and sentence constructions to be used in my writings.

* * *

In this book, Croma is a ship. For the description of its interiors and the rhythm of life on board, I used the trans-atlantic ship Augustus as a model.

Many have asked why I gave the ship the name of Croma and used it in the title.

As a child I was enthralled with the history of Rome and its founding by Romulus and Remus. I thought then that I might one day found such a city in the region of Mato Grosso and that I would give it the name of Croma.

Preparing to write, this book, I recalled this episode while searching through my reminiscences. While I obviously have not yet founded a city, here, notwithstanding, is the book: *Croma*.

THE AUTHOR

Chapter I

Torres is boarding a cruise ship for the first time. His old dream has come true, and his satisfaction is reflected in his face. His eyes dart everywhere, taking in each detail with curiosity.

He goes to the reception desk, hands on over his bag, receives his cabin and dining room assignments, and goes up to the deck at dockside because he wants to see the Port of the Santos.

A seagull glides over the water just slightly above the ship. Its flights sustained with delicate movements of the wings and the head hangs low, searching the marine depths.

Torres looks up, more accustomed to the horizons of the seminary, to absorb the breadth of the new horizon. After a while, pleased with the scene, he goes down to his cabin and opening the door, encounters the gentleman with whom he will be sharing the compartment.

"Pleased to meet you, Alvaro Ruiz."

"The pleasure is all mine, Fernando Torres."

"I was a little concerned when I learned that a priest would take the place of my wife."

"Why?"

"Since your clothes are somewhat similar to hers, I was afraid you might restrain my life somewhat," he says, breaking into a hearty laugh. "Don't take that as a put down. Fortunately, you're a young priest, and we'll be able to have some frank discussions; older priests are much too set in their ways."

"I'm not yet a priest. I finished the seminary just last month."

"So you haven't yet been ordained?"

"I have five months to reflect upon the responsibilities of the priesthood."

"Interesting, very interesting! And if, in that time, you realize that you do not have the calling, you'll be able to leave the seminary without difficulty. Right?"

"Yes, but if I could, I would have been ordained already, even though it would have interfered with this prize trip to Rome."

"Don't be in too much of hurry, young man, you have plenty of time for that; the orientation of the church is very wise. Well, do you want to sleep in the upper or the lower?"

"I don't care."

"Well, if you don't mind, I would prefer to place my 198 pounds down below."

The loudspeaker in corridor sounds the first call to lunch.

"Let's go to lunch; we can unpack the bags later," says Ruiz.

"You lead the way."

"You're the oldest, you should go first…"

"Never mind that, you go ahead."

The tables in the dining room of the Croma are placed in a semicircle. The waiter, an Italian of few words but with rapid and precise movements, serves them soup without paying any attention to the linguistic extravagance of Ruiz.

10

Beef, potatoes and vegetables are already on their plates. Savoring the food makes further conversation difficult.

The ship remains anchored in the port of Santos. The loudspeaker announces, from one moment to the next, that all visitors must leave the ship, and constant reminders by crew members reflect the excitement of departure.

"Let's finish lunch quickly and go on deck to wave good-bye," proposes Ruiz.

"Very well."

"A little more wine? It's pretty weak," he says, tipping the bottle into Torres' glass.

"But, as I was saying, my wife had to stay with our children... her mother became ill at the last moment. That's a lie – she's useless even for watching over the children. Poor Lucia – she missed a good opportunity to see Europe."

"Will you be staying long in Europe?"

"Two to three months. I'm going to a congress in Switzerland and then I will take a course in France."

"What's your specialty?"

"Psychiatry – I'm the director of a governmental psychiatric hospital."

"Ah!..."

"Pay no attention to my manners, madness is highly contagious," he comments, breaking out again in noisy laughter.

What a wonderful trip I'm going to have! thinks Torres.

He is somewhat taken aback by the continued extroversion of the doctor. His lack of contact with the world, due to his isolation in the seminary, has made him feel inhibited.

"Can't you use any other clothes, like a clerical suit?"

"Yes, I can."

"Then why do you prefer that long skirt. The clerical suit is easier to pack."

He is tempted to make a sharp response, but religious training prevents his taking such an attitude. He is, he recognizes sadly, at the mercy of the doctor's jibes.

"Are you finished? Then let's go."

Torres rises and, with a quick glance, instinctively looks for any spots on the white cassock. The doctor notices this and his mocking smile makes him blush again.

On deck, crowded with people, the loudspeaker calls out last minute messages and some sailors run from one side to the other.

The dock remains packed with friends and relatives. The last gangplank is quickly removed and three blows on the whistle shrill through the air. The noise of the crowd increases; a few serpentines are thrown and handkerchiefs wave good-bye.

The tugboat goes to work, and the gap between ship and dock starts increasing. Lines are released, the tugboat whistles departure, the ship responds, and the bow of the ship begins to cut through the water.

Santos, off to the right, moves slowly away. At the docks, ships of various nationalities are lined up. One of them signals a greeting with three long whistles. Some sailors wave from the deck; the Italian flag flutters from the stern. The Croma answers, frightening the passengers. Speed increases as they cross over the bar. They have sailed. A long and melancholy whistle breaks over the horizon and, ahead of them, sea and sky come together.

"Are you going below?" asks Ruiz.

"No, I think I'll stay here a while longer."

"Well, I'm going to unpack. See you later."

"See you."

The July sky is blue and cloudless, and the southerly wind, laden with salty drops of water fogs over Torres' glasses. The waves break against the ship with characteristic sounds, and seagulls shrill as they wheel above it.

Torres breathes deeply, and the salt air fills his lungs, refreshing them. From where he stands, he can see only the sea, and on the other side the continent passing by. His fertile imagination momentarily breaks through all that water and comes to rest on the sands of Africa.

"Five hundred years ago," he thinks, "the first caravels passed by here." Almost instinctively he looks up and sees the great funnel expelling smoke and noise.

The ship's stabilizers allow it to glide smoothly through the waters; it is an enormous moving bathtub.

The vibration of the motors reminds him to go down to take his seasick pills.

"The steward left this key for you," says Ruiz.

"Thank you."

"Shall we get acquainted? How old are you?"

"Twenty-seven."

"A good age. I'm forty-nine. Did you enter the seminary very young?"

"I was nineteen."

"That's not very common, is it?"

"No," answers Torres, hanging up his few unpacked clothes.

"What strange reasons would lead a young man of that age into the seminary?" he whispers.

"Are you asking a question?"

"No, just thinking."

Having finished arranging his clothes, Torres closes his suitcase and places it in a corner. He opens the closet and, taking out a gray clerical suit, goes into the bathroom. Moments later he returns to the cabin. The white cassock is hanging from a hanger.

"Well, well?" exclaims the doctor, looking him over. "Now you're beginning to looking like a normal guy. Take off the collar for a moment."

"Why?"

"I want to see you in ordinary clothes."

The younger man figures it will be easier to take off the collar than to question it, so he does.

"A normal fellow, perfectly normal."

Torres, somewhat bothered with these irrelevancies, decides he will stay out of the cabin as much as possible.

"Where are you going?"

"Up above."

"Again! Wait, don't be upset like that. Excuse my indiscretions and sit down here."

He sits down reluctantly.

"Let's talk seriously now. I think that I am, like you, an idealist. I could have left the hospital long ago and set up my own office to treat high society neurotics. One of my colleagues offered to go into partnership with me."

He takes a cigarette from a pack on the table.

"Do you smoke?"

"No, thank you."

"I thought a lot before turning down the offer. Today he is a prosperous psychoanalyst. His office is modern and well-decorated. Believe me, he has three nurses – three! His

14

clients pay $150 for weekly or biweekly consultations over a long period of time. It's a gold mine!"

"Are you sorry?"

"Sorry? I really don't know – sometimes my material dreams end up in financial difficulties, and sometimes I have moments of satisfaction with a job well done. Although I'm not steadfastly religious, I believe we have a duty to fulfill with the rest of humanity."

"There was a time in my life when I wanted to become a psychiatrist like you."

"Tell me what happened."

"Maybe another time."

"Very well. Interesting, I've never had a priest in my hands. An aged nun once as a patient, but never a priest."

"We have our own methods," he says proudly.

"Your own methods? And what might they be?"

"God. Those who belong to Him body and soul have no need of the couch."

"I respect your opinion. But are all of you really aware of what you are doing?"

"What do you mean by that?"

"Isn't frustration responsible for the priesthood?"

"One needs much more than frustration to belong to God."

"I won't argue against that, but I would like to see some evidence of this predestination."

Torres thinks to himself, not with me, although I can imagine what he's driving at!

"If you will excuse me, I'm going out."

"As you wish."

Torres had reacted like any seminarian. He could not permit that someone should doubt his faith, and he received these presentations as an unforgivable intrusion.

The number of passengers on the bridge was small for that time of day. The excitement of departure and unpacking clothes had kept them in their cabins.

Making the rounds of the deck, he passes by the empty pool and sits down in one of the lounge chairs. At his side, some people are reading. The sea in front of him stretches out endlessly and, on the other side, the continent is a small gray speck. The cold wind continues to invigorate his lungs, and the noise of the waves crashing against the ship makes him drowsy.

Looking to his left, he sees some newspapers scattered about on top of small table. He rises and picks up a copy. At a glance, he can see that it is printed in three languages: Italian, Spanish and Portuguese. It gives an idea about the ship as a whole: focuses on passengers of Brazilian nationality. On the backside is the daily program. Pool, games on the bridge, movies, etc... Tired of reading, he folds the newspaper and casts his eyes over the deck.

"Could you lend me the paper?" asks a young girl at his side.

"Of course."

The eyes of the girl lock on his, disconcerting him.

"Thank you," she says with a friendly smile.

"You're welcome."

Turning, he instinctively raises his hand to his neck. He realizes he is not wearing the collar!

A normal fellow, perfectly normal, he remembers Ruiz saying.

16

Not knowing what to do, he gets up and begins to wander aimlessly about the deck. The number of passengers has grown, and the murmur of voices reflects animation and arouses curiosity. The number of girls and women is greater than that of men.

After some time he goes to the chapel and kneels in one of the pews. Two priests on his left are praying the breviary. He recalls again that he is without the collar; it's the first time in many years that he has entered a church without the complete outfit of a priest. He can't concentrate on his prayers; he feels like a different person.

A normal fellow, perfectly normal.

"Back so soon?" asks Ruiz, lying down.

"I forgot my collar and came back to get it."

"Why don't you leave it off? Are you afraid?"

"Afraid... of what?"

Torres had intended to stay in the cabin, but he is overcome by a strange feeling of repulsion.

"Where are you going?"

"To the chapel."

"Why not rest a bit. Take off your jacket and shoes. If you like, I'll go above."

"You needn't bother," he says, taking off his jacket.

"There, isn't that better?" says Ruiz after a while.

"Yes."

"Do you want to talk?"

Torres would rather meditate on his emotions and find out just what bothered him so much.

"If you like," he answers, politely.

The porthole is at his side. He turns toward it and lets himself rise and fall with the waves. The sky is still blue, and the wind blows salty drops against the glass. The vibration of the ship rocks him leisurely. He closes his eyes and sleeps.

Two hours later he is awakened by an announcement from the loudspeaker.

"To all passengers: tea is now being served in the dining room," is announced in all three languages.

"Are you going to tea?" asks Ruiz.

"Yes."

A feeling of well-being runs through his body, and he stretches lazily. He goes into the bathroom and enters the shower. The force of the water reinvigorates his muscles and the temperature is delightful.

"Let's go, or we'll miss tea," says Ruiz, knocking on the door a few minutes later.

He turns off the water and picks up a towel. His uneasiness with the doctor almost forgotten.

The tea room is the same as that for lunch. Few persons want food at that hour. Games on the bridge, the pool and cinema have absorbed the attention of the passengers.

Tea, toast, crackers and slices of cheese are laid out on the table. They help themselves.

"While you were sleeping, I was making up a test for you."

"For me?!"

"Yes. It's going to be a long voyage, and this is a wonderful opportunity to test your vocation."

"I don't understand."

"Let me explain. You seminarians are, like all of us, human beings, and you are, therefore, subject to animal instincts. But the exercise of self-control to which you submit yourself eliminates these impulses."

18

"And where is the harm in that?"

"It's that you are impeded from definitively testing your vocation. Your conscience behaves under managed thinking, somewhat like conditioned reflexes. Any doubts or temptations are repelled as imminent sin. Sin is associated with the confessional, and the confessional means humiliation, self-condemnation and punishment."

"True Christians, as believers, have the moral obligation to resist temptation," answers Torres with complete certainty.

"These temptations, frequently, do not signify sin, and if you seminarians, now and then, would give them the benefit of the doubt, you would lose your fear."

"Fear of what?"

"Fear of examining yourselves, of confronting reality, and, finally, of losing yourselves in your beliefs. This doesn't mean losing yourselves, but rather finding yourselves. If, in fact, your faith is as solid as a rock, nothing can upset it. But if you run away from the fight like cowards and hide behind convenient clothing, how can you be sure of the degree of your faith?"

"And just what is the basis for this conclusion insofar as I am concerned?"

"Your clerical collar."

"Humpf!"

"When you came into the cabin and said: 'I came to get my collar,' your eyes showed anguish and despair. You were like a knight of the crusades without his armor. How would you deflect the arrows and axes without this shield?"

"Might it not be that you are trying to lead me to what you psychologists call directed thought?"

"Not this time, no. I admit having used that device for a long time. Your church is wise to give you five months to

19

meditate about your vocation, and this opportunity should not be wasted. It may be the only one you will ever have. The test will either strengthen your priestly spirit or lead you to give up the cassock. In the future you will remember all this with pleasure, and what I am proposing to you will not damage your religious beliefs."

They get up and go on deck. With some difficulty they find two chairs. They sit down.

"What kind of a test is this, after all?"

"A romance or, better yet, love."

"What you're suggesting is ridiculous."

"That's where you're wrong. Without these clothes you are transformed into a normal fellow."

Some young girls in swim suits pass by them and look at him with curiosity. Torres, instinctively, raises his hands to his collar; he has it on, and a smile of relief bursts across his lips.

"I don't think you understand my vocation. As far as I'm concerned, I have already taken my perpetual vows as a religious."

"You are mistaken; everything has its own natural order: first, doubt; and then, certainty. Do not be afraid, even if, in the end, you still feel frustration, you will be able to give up human desires conscientiously and take your final vows as a religious."

Torres, from what little he knows of Ruiz, decides to give in to the idea. It will be easier to beat him this way rather than constantly interrupt him with arguments. The doctor won't give up easily, and Torres wants to have a peaceful voyage.

"How would we carry out this test?"

"Now you're being a sensible fellow. You will stop wearing the collar and vest, and we will buy some sports shirts, some shorts, and you will travel as a well off bachelor 27 years old. We will look for an interesting guinea pig who will introduce you to the flames of love and carry out the test. Love *versus* vocation, and non-love *versus* God. Let it be understood: you must remember this premise. It is love *versus* the standards of religious life. Don't develop a guilt complex about faith before you even begin, understand?"

"I think so."

"Do you agree, then?"

"I don't know. I'll have to meditate a good deal before making a decision". No other answer was be possible.

"I'll give you until dinnertime."

"That's all?"

"That's enough."

"If you'll excuse me, I'm going for a walk," Torres says, getting up.

"All right... wait a minute: a short while ago I saw you raise your hand to your collar when those girls in swimsuits walked by. Were you raising it to your shield?"

"Well... I don't know."

"Meditate on it, then."

The movement of passengers had grown considerably. Torres walks rapidly past the pool, crowded with people, and heads for the deck opposite to Ruiz.

From a distance, the continent is still just a gray and uniform mass.

The young man loses all sense of time in meditation. The call "Signori Passageri..." startles him.

The loudspeaker sounds the calls in loud volume. Already accustomed to the polyglot manifestations of the announcements, he only listens to the one in his own language.

"All passengers, dinner is served in the Dining Salon for those who hold assignments for the first sitting."

He looks at the card he received on boarding and heads toward the Dining Salon as directed.

Ruiz receives him effusively. The dialog which follows reveals a certain indifference to the theme discussed in the afternoon, and the doctor intends to make him feel at ease. A little later, he returns to the subject.

"Have you meditated on the test?"

"All afternoon."

"And what is your answer?"

Torres, when he was on the deck, had been trying to figure out something that would ensure him a peaceful voyage. *To conquer an adversary, use his own weapons against him.*"

"I agree with you, but there is one condition."

"Condition?"

"You have psychological experience, and you know that psychic diagnosis of a person depends upon his past. In knowing the innermost secrets of your patients, you discover and bring out obscure facts, isn't that so?"

"That's true, but what are you driving at?"

"I propose to tell you about my life. If, when I have finished my story in detail, you decide that I should make this test, I will accept."

"But that's not necessary, in your case…"

"You have never treated a case without knowing the past, and I certainly will not let mine be an exception."

The young man is emboldened and feels capable of opposing the doctor's insistent impertinence.

"You are clever, aren't you, hoping to gain some time?"

"I, that is... of course not. You have no idea about my vocation without knowing everything about my life."

"And the collar?"

"That proves nothing. It was an isolated incident, a conditioned reflex."

"I'm beginning to like you. If you had reacted differently like... like an old, stuffy priest: 'That would be a sin' or 'God help me!' I would have lost interest in pursuing the matter. But the rules are laid out... I agree, but with one other condition."

"Which is?"

"Your life story will take up too much of the time necessary to conclude the test. I suggest you start the test at the same time as you begin telling me about your past. Then, if, at the end of your story, I verify the existence of an irreversible priestly vocation, we'll give up the test. All right?"

Ruiz was being astute, but he could not have hoped for anything else. Torres, with his naïve ingenuity, had thought that he might be able to distract him. He felt it impossible to refuse the counter proposal in the light of twenty years of psychiatric experience. The doctor might think up other arguments, other obscure reasons and would end up either convincing him or committing him to the government sanitarium as its first interned seminarian.

The pitcher of wine is running low. Ruiz serves himself and the young man amply. The loudspeaker announces:

"All passengers, we will arrive in Rio at 2200 hours. A delegation of the Mangueira Samba School will come aboard and begin our carnival ball. Please dress in costume and go to the Sala Feste and Sala Soggiorno.

"This is a good time to start the test," comments Ruiz, euphorically.

"How so?"

"We'll check out all the *femmes fatales*, and you'll have to choose a young lady who has all the qualities needed for the test. She must be sufficiently close to your feminine ideal, or even better, the poetic ideal you had before you entered the seminary. Do you have any suggestions?"

"No, none" – the wine has had its effect.

"Then let's get up and waste no time. As we walk on deck, you can begin to tell me about your life."

They go up on deck.

The sun sets slowly. The water, embellished with red, contrasts with the darker sky and the quavering stars. Yet another cycle has come to an end. The ship continues to vibrate from the throbbing of the engines, and a cool, salty breeze tosses their hair as though caressing it.

"Our activities, with a few differences, will be the same" says Torres. "My couch will be the confessional where I will relive the dramas of my psyche. I shall be pursued, like you, by the most diverse convictions, and for them I shall have a response."

"Let's go, then, young man. Tell me your past as quick as you can, and use no subterfuges," advises Ruiz, frustrating any attempt to stray from the theme.

The sun has disappeared completely by now. But a few story rays block the light from the still emerging stars.

Chapter II

Torres was six pink and happy years old, just like all children at this age. It was a day like any other, and it was recess time in the kindergarten of the School of the Angels in Botucatu (a small town in the interior of the State of São Paulo, Brazil). He was perched near a corner of the building, a solitary observer of his playmates who were playing in the courtyard. This aloofness was the result of a conversation with sister Theresa.

"You are such a quiet, somber little boy that you would make a good priest," as the white hand with the long fingers slid through his curly hair in a caress.

He felt a chill run through his body, and he blushed deeply when she fixed her eyes on him and repeated:

"You would make a good priest."

"A priest? Me?"

He quickly associated the idea of the priesthood with cassocks, quietude and sadness.

I think I'll be priest...

I'm gonna be priest..., he concludes, imagining himself walking with dark cloth swirling about him.

Suddenly an uncontrollable desire took hold of him. He wanted to run and tell his decision to sister Theresa,

25

and for the rest of the day his attention seized upon this fact. When school was over, he took the last place in line and, as he passed the sister at the gate, he blurted out the project he had been turning over in his mind.

"I'm gonna be priest."

"So, my earnest little man, you want to be a priest?!" she exclaimed, running her fingers once again through his hair.

"Yeah, I'm gonna be priest."

"Very well, I'll make you into a priest, then. Now run along home. Wait a minute," she called after him, "your pants have split the seam."

He looked behind him: his pants had split open nearly two inches. Embarrassed, he began to pick up speed. The priesthood was no longer his only concern. He stopped only when he reached the corner, nearly two blocks from the school. With all the running, his pants had opened up even more. He looked down the street and spotted his house; he looked up the street: no-one; to each side: no-one. The cold sweat on his temples was wiped with nimble fingers. He could felt a thousand smiling, cynical faces looking at him. There was nowhere to hide, and he begged for the ground to open up beneath him and swallow him.

"I'm all alone," he reasoned, looking around once again.

He began to walk, but stopped after a few steps. He looked to both sides: no-one. He started out again, normally. When he reached his house at the opposite side from the gate, he saw the neighbor across from him reading his newspaper on the front porch; he was sitting in a rocking chair, rocking back and forth incessantly. He stopped and stared to see if he was being observed out the corner of his eye. No, no he wasn't. As he started down the last stretch, he was startled by a sudden feeling. The man had lowered the newspaper to turn around and look him.

Torres backed up against the wall, parallel to the street; he tried to hide the tear in his pants.

"How are you?"

"O... OK," he answered, crossing his hands behind him.

He couldn't move, and the man continued looking at him.

Could he have seen it? he wondered, terrified.

The neighbor turned his attention back to the newspaper, and Torres entered quickly, slamming the iron gate behind him.

"Mom, mom!" he ran screaming. Finding her, he stopped, out of breath. "Mom, I tore my pants."

Without saying anything, she took off his pants and dressed him in another pair. The boy cheered up.

"Be more careful next time."

"OK. I'm gonna be priest."

"A priest? Why?"

"The sister said I looked like a priest."

"It's a little early yet. We'll see after a while."

"I wanna be priest," he began to whimper, "the sister said..."

"When you're a little older..."

"No, I wanna be, now."

"Well, you can't right now," she said as she finished straightening up his clothes.

Torres left the bathroom running in the direction of the backyard. Outside, he picked up a stick and began to walk aimlessly, hitting any object he came across. Tears ran down his face. The incident with his pants and the emotion of the afternoon, together with his mother's negation made him desperate.

He didn't want to disappoint the one who ran her fingers through his hair. In his innocence, he had thought that he could go immediately to the seminary. He was afraid of the world, and his fear of what lay ahead increased his desire to isolate himself.

* * *

"You were hardly aware, then, that the two facts were interrelated and that, if she had asked you to be a thief, you would be one," intrudes Ruiz. "But perhaps you really did have a predisposition toward the priesthood at that time. This psychoanalytic mania of mine can twist certain facts when they are seen only through a Freudian prism. Go on."

Torres, a beginner wine drinker during the voyage, was already feeling its effect. An acrid taste rose up in his throat; he was definitely not a drinker. He pays little attention to the intrusion and continues with his story.

* * *

Over the next few days he enjoyed a fertile and mystic friendship with the nun. She saw in that small boy the accomplishment of her dream as a religious educator. The hope of attending the ordination of one of her students rested in him.

Catechism classes were individual and took place for an hour every two days.

Young Sister Theresa wore a habit that fell straight down to her feet and a wimple like an upside down U that framed her mystic smile. Her natural and pleasantly didactic appearance set her apart from the other nuns because it was motivated by the simple fact that she was fond of him. He saw her as the fairy godmother from the tale he had heard recently of Cinderella.

Torres received the Christian teachings with avid enthusiasm. While the Nun impassively revealed all of the doctrines, the eyes of the boy remained ecstatic and wide open.

"In the beginning, God created the heavens and the earth," she said, instructing him in the theism of Genesis.

"And how did He make heaven and earth show up?" he inquired timidly.

"He can do anything."

"And... He..." he stammered.

"Go ahead and ask," she encouraged him in a friendly manner.

"If I want, can he give me ice cream and chocolate?"

"Yes, He could," she answered patiently. "Let's continue."

While Genesis was being elaborated on, Torres was still concerned with ice cream and chocolate.

"And the evening and the morning were the fourth day. Now, repeat the first three days."

"Repeat what?"

"What I just told you!"

"You said that He made heaven and earth and the ocean, too?"

"The ocean, too," she agrees, sweetly, "and what else?"

"You said He can give ice cream and chocolate."

"No, not that."

"You said so!"

"All right... Let's go on to the days of the creation."

Genesis was explained, and with it was born the gluttonous suggestion of divine benevolence. The uncertainties would end only when the ice cream and chocolate offered by God had arrived.

Sister Theresa, with her inexhaustible ecclesiastical virtues, went over the plans for the future priest at every opportunity.

At the age of seven, after piously receiving his first communion, Torres was separated from the one who ran her fingers through his hair. And when his admission to the seminary was decided for his tenth birthday, this separation became final.

The ceremony of the first communion was a solemn one. White suit, candle in his hand and most holy aspirations. The Host that he received contained God.

After the religious service, a table of sweets awaited the new disciples, and there, among other things, were ice cream and chocolate.

The following year, he attended the same ceremony in the same suit. An attractive group of boys and girls occupied the front pews. As they left the church, he joined them. His frightened little head spun around as he searched for reproving glances. Minutes later he was again at the side of the table of sweets. This deed made him, by virtue of his innocence, in debt with God.

Mass was attended with deep devotion. He became imbued with the idea of the priesthood, and he prayed at Mass with a friend who had the same intention.

* * *

While his plans were becoming more detailed, a family moved into the house across the street. In this family there was a young girl nine years old like him.

Silvia, with black hair and hazel eyes, quick as a little monkey, seduced him from the very start. Within a short time, he was a frequent visitor to the house. At the time he was unaware of the meaning of the verb 'to impose.'

Mary, her mother, reminded him of the Mother of Jesus, both because she had the same name and because of the simple compassion that exuded from her delicate body. She had a constant smile that forgave even the most serious misbehavior. He never met her father for the simple reason that his visits coincided with the time when he was away at work.

He remembered, with a smile on his lips, of the little secrets in the backyard. They became 'boyfriend' and 'girlfriend' by virtue of the fact that they had sat together at the movies. At that time, this fact could substitute the uncomfortable formality commonly practiced.

Silvia was his first willing love. Her wishes were laws and her charms, shackles that imprisoned him.

Torres' legs took him to see her daily, and his little heart, with its rhythmic beat, was now accelerated with the nourishment of her affection.

The days became months and the months, years. During the whole time, he had to pay heavy tribute for that love. The whims of his young and faithful companion came to assume dangerous proportions; it was necessary to be courageous and to be ready to take on lions with a brave heart.

Once, when he wanted to sit with her at the movies, he had to climb over a 13 foot high wall and jump into a pile of sand on the other side.

He accepted the challenge, climbed up and sat on the top, fearful of falling. He couldn't manage the jump; he was frozen to the wall and she hooted, sneering at his lack of courage.

"It's too high; I can't do it," he said, after long minutes of timid attempts.

"If you don't jump, I'll call Joey and, if he jumps, I'll sit with him at the movies."

Joey, a friend and rival, had started, months ago, to make advances toward her. They had already clashed twice because of her. Silvia was delighted with this rivalry. Nevertheless, it was always Torres who sat with her at the movies. The reason for this preference, perhaps, was because he always walked with her as if he were glued to her.

Time passed and no courage came to his aid. The girl jumped and rolled around in the sand, smiling facetiously. Her jibes struck directly into his soul, and he adored her at that moment. His fear, however, kept him from proving his passion. A half hour had gone by when, about to give up, she shouted:

"Wait! Don't come down. Wait a little."

Torres saw her run quickly to the fence and shout for Joey. Moments later they were at the foot of the wall. She whispered something into the ear of his friend who slowly climbed up to be at his side.

"Whoever jumps first can sit with me at the movies."

Torres looked with alarm at his companion; Joey didn't even acknowledge his presence. Suddenly Joey launched himself into space and fell softly, with his arms wide open, on the pile of sand.

"Hooray for Joey! He did it! You're not a man, you're not a man!" she shouted, taunting him.

His heart was shattered. His rival got up and brushed himself off, enjoying every moment of his feat.

He had no other alternative but to jump. He jumped. As he fell, a cold chill ran through his body from head to heels. A deafening thump as he struck the sand signaled journey's end. He opened his eyes, looked about, and, head down, began to clean off his hands and trousers.

He felt a terrible defeat. He had an urge to grab his rival and prove by fighting which one of the two was the better man. But he was frozen to the spot.

Silvia was talking with Joey and paid no attention to him. He realized, humiliated, that he couldn't stay there a moment longer. He left.

He left, fantasizing a desire to throw himself at her feet, asking forgiveness, and making passionate overtures. This scene, which he had seen in a recent film, had impressed him.

As he reached the gate to leave, she called out to him.

"Hey, wait a minute!" she said, running. "If you give me a dollar, I'll sit with you at the movies."

His piggy bank appeared in his mind and he calculated how much was in it.

"OK, I will."

"Wait for me at the same place, but don't sit down until the lights go out."

He agreed and left with his head held high, his masculinity completely restored.

That night he paid her, and, in order to hold her hand lovingly, he paid her another dollar.

What would be your reaction if you were the innocent victim of these feminine wiles? Well, that's exactly what happened, he couldn't leave her side. He gave her candy, he sent her Valentine's Day and birthday cards. She treated him like a doormat, and each time she wiped her feet on him, he kissed them with love.

Torres' life went on like this until he was ten, and he was well aware that priests could not marry. His childish mind brooded on the path to be followed. The muse who ruined priestly vocations demanded total surrender.

* * *

"At that time, were you having any qualms of conscience?" asks Ruiz with growing interest.

* * *

Torres had learned in catechism class that divine plans must always be carried out under penalty of condemnation to the fires of hell, and he considered himself to be predestined to the service of God.

His heart leaned toward the girl and in his innocence, he felt, guilty and deserving of the roaring flames. He was terrified at the idea of being roasted over a slow fire spitted upon a three pointed fork. He began to experience a certain strange warmth.

* * *

"That is exactly what was one of the main errors of Catholicism," interrupts Ruiz, "the Council knowingly substituted a religion of fear with that of love. Clergymen, responsible for the religious instruction of children, thought it necessary to instill these ideas precisely because that is the phase of life when the psychic formation of the human being occurs. They had taught, then, the concepts of good and evil, love and hate. Now, they needed to stress that evil is the absence of good and not the reverse."

* * *

When Torres completed his tenth year, the age at which he was to enter the seminary, he wanted to marry her. With that decision came a guilt complex, because of the religious doctrine he had learned. He continued going to mass but without feeling the mystic flashes as before. At the start of the service, he only thought of when it would end, and he continued to fear divine punishment.

* * *

"Your hell fire was nothing more than a punishment, where the one being punished assumes the despair and withdraw intended by the one punishing. But the commandments of your Church can be summed up as to love God above all other things and to love your neighbor as yourself. What were your feelings, at that time, toward your neighbor?"

* * *

At first, Torres could not understand why some had so much and others had so little. He had no knowledge of either selfishness or hatred, with an occasional exception for Joey.

How that little infantile heart suffered upon feeling the poverty of his colleagues! Indigence could be seen in the bare feet and ragged, but always clean, clothes. The hungry looks staring at the lunches of the rich boys revealed an inborn and constant hunger. The envy and the denial of apples, chocolates and sodas transformed them into humiliated and depressed human beings.

The smarter ones invented ways to satisfy their uncontained desires. They suggested to the richer boys that they share their lunch. They would nearly always exchange a piece of hard bread for a bite of apple or fresh bread with cheese or jam. Torres shared his lunch with two or three friends. Sunday afternoons he would go to the movies and, when he met up with some friend without any money at the door, he would pay for his ticket.

His colleagues at this time were divided into three categories. Those who wore shoes, those who had only one shoe, and those who had no shoes. The majority always walked with one shoe. The other foot, shoeless, was the one that 'really hurt.' The following week the shoeless foot would heal and get the shoe while the other 'got hurt' and went shoeless. Torres wanted to be like them and, sometimes, he 'hurt one of his feet.' He was proud to be part of the majority, which was the very picture of underdevelopment.

When he turned 11, contrary to his desire of three years back, he did not go into the seminary: he left that decision to after grade school because, despite everything, he still felt a strange attraction for the priesthood.

Chapter III

"Let's get dressed for the dance," suggests Ruiz.

Torres reluctantly changes his clerical suit for a sports shirt and trousers. The bathroom mirror reflects the change in outfit. The priestly clothes hanging behind the door take on the aspect of his spiritual supervisor. His awareness of the empty clothes reproaches him.

The shirt borrowed from the doctor is a little large, but 'today is Carnival,' as his friend had said upon seeing him distraught. Torres takes on his enthusiasm like a robot.

"Dr. Ruiz, let's not go so fast," begs the young man.

"Have no fear, you have everything to gain, you may be sure. The body is perfect, and how is the soul doing?"

"Not so well. I'm really feeling indiscreet about this."

"Let's bare your soul, then. My experience tells me that the period that you're going through is really important."

"What do you mean?"

"I'll explain: between the ages of 28 and 32, man feels a generalized doubt. Everything is confusing, nothing seems to make sense, and he is desperately searching for a purpose in life. When he sees older men, he puts himself in their place, studies the past, and feels how transitory everything is. After much tribulation, concrete doubt overtakes him. It's a crossroads."

"Suppose that this crossroads that you refer to occurred during my university days, during my choice of profession."

"No, my dear fellow, at that age we are not capable of definitive solutions, only transitory ones. We'll cover Platonic love during our second stroll. Now let's go to the dance."

Torres can feel that the doctor is tearing down his final resistance. The vivid scenes pass all too quickly and allow him little time for deeper study.

The *Sala Feste* and the *Sala Soggiorno* are decorated with serpentines and glitter. The Mangueira Samba School has already arrived. The distinctive rhythm of the tambourines and cuicas (the cuica is a drum-like instrument, open at one end and with a stick attached to the drumhead which, when rubbed, gives off a high-pitched squeaking sound) enliven the salon. Revelers and women walking in step with the rhythm go from table to table, encouraging the shy passengers. The costumes are varied and picturesque.

From a corner of the room, Torres and the doctor, spot the revelers letting loose with exclamations and gestures. The cheerfulness is contagious. Ruiz accompanies the rhythm with his body and his hands.

"Cheer up!" he shouts over the noise of the crowd.

The younger man still hangs back a little. There is still the shadow of a doubt which gradually is undermined by the general enthusiasm. After a while, he smiles and begins to tap his foot to the rhythm in the ballroom.

Eight years before, he had abandoned these pagan manifestations in order to live in mystic seclusion, and how happy he had been during all that time! Contemplation and the absence of immediate concerns had transformed his theory of life. The possessions of the spirit had received primary importance.

Now he had accepted the test outlined by the doctor, and he must do it perfectly so there could be no future doubts.

"Look, the women now outnumber the men both in number and spirit. Just look at the exuberance of those girls!"

Torres begins to examine the appearance of the girls. Their smiles make him feel like a recently cured blind man, everything seems strange and exciting.

Suddenly, a group of four girls approaches them with obvious intentions. The young man gives a startled look at the doctor. The girls arrive and take them by the hand.

"Come on, let's go into the ballroom," they shout, as they continue to step to the rhythm.

"We can't," answers Ruiz, taking the initiative.

"Why? Are you married?" shouts one of them.

"Yes, we're married."

"Oh, what a shame!" they say, almost in unison.

They leave and go to the dance floor, dancing all the way.

"Thanks. I..."

"Shh! Be quiet and keep watching the faces."

> *"Oh, little gardener, why are you so sad?*
> *What happened to you?"*
> *"It was a camellia that fell from its branch,*
> *sighed twice, and died."*
> *"Come, little gardener, come, my love.*
> *Be not sad, for the world is all yours.*

You are far more beautiful
than the camellia that died."

The eternal "Little Gardener" is responsible for the climax of the ball. There isn't a single Brazilian who doesn't sing it. Torres becomes caught up in the enthusiasm and happily joins in the singing.

It's two in the morning when the samba school leaves the ship. The more enthusiastic revelers go with them to the dock, and their electrifying rhythm fades into the distance.

"All passengers, we are now opening the night club in the *Sala Feste*. We hope you will all have a good time."

The lights become diffuse and indirect, reflecting a typical night club atmosphere. Slow and romantic music is accompanied by the voice of a singer. Couples in love dance cheek to cheek.

"Shall we turn in?" says Ruiz, yawning widely.

"Yes, let's," he agrees, sleepily.

"Tomorrow we shall begin the search for our guinea pig," he explains on the way to the cabin.

At ten o'clock the next morning, Torres, pulls aside the curtains of the porthole and sees the waves crashing against the hull of the ship. The ship had already sailed from Rio, bound for Lisbon.

"How can these sailors work on a day like this?" he thinks, taking a stretch.

He slowly climbs down from his bunk. Ruiz is still asleep, and he doesn't want to wake him. The program for the day had been slipped under the door. He picks it up, reads a few paragraphs, then goes into the bathroom.

A hot shower re-invigorates him pleasantly as his conscience deliberates his defense.

40

...I don't see anything wrong. Let's get on with the test. God will understand, he concludes, tranquilizing himself.

The sea grows rougher, and the air is impregnated with salt spray. Stepping out of the shower, he wraps a towel around himself and looks in the fogged over mirror. A smile breaks out on his face. He knows how important these moments are to his life, and he wants to live them intensely. While dressing, he feels that his personality is being decked out in new clothes. Going back into the cabin, he comes face to face with Ruiz, already up.

"How are you?" asks the doctor.

"Fine."

"The shops are open, and we need to buy some clothes. I'll take a shower, and we can go."

"I'll go up on deck and wait for you at the same place as yesterday."

"Don't forget to size up the girls in detail," he says, with a knowing smile.

There are few passengers on deck at that hour. Middle-aged couples stroll contentedly. The younger passengers are still in their cabins. There will be another ball that night, and their strength needs to be renewed for the dance 'marathon.'

The south wind blows, cooling him, and the sky is still cloudless.

Torres rests his gaze upon the horizon. His mind, eager for knowledge, races across the ocean a head of the ship and comes to rest on the sands of Africa. There, his mind's eye sees a native girl bathing in the foaming surf...

After a while, tired of the same position, he goes to the other side of the ship to see the continent. Brazil is no longer there! It has been swept away and in its place is only water.

41

He steps away from the rail and sits down in one of the lounge chairs. He is incapable, through years of habit, of remaining seated without reading. He looks around for the ship's newspaper. A little off to the right there is a small table with a few copies. He gets up, crosses in front of some passengers stretched out in their chairs, and sits down next to the table.

"Italy?" asks a young lady who is nearby.

The young man, in his haste to get the newspaper, had not noticed her presence.

"What?" he says, alarmed.

"I asked if you are going to Italy," she replies, simultaneously closing the book in her hands.

"Yes, I'm going to Italy," he answers, calming down.

She takes off her glasses and tucks up her legs which had been extended the length of the chair; her body assumes a comfortable posture. Her face harmonizes with her black hair, and her clean features, with almost no make-up, let an enormous compassion show through the delicate outlines. She is not a raving beauty; however, a tranquil mellowness emanates from her. Her well manicured hands demonstrate femininity.

"Is this your first voyage?"

"Yes, the first time."

"This is my second voyage."

"Oh!" he mumbles awkwardly. He doesn't know what to say or where to put his hands.

"These trips, if you can't manage to find some company, can be very monotonous."

"I guess so."

"Did you go to the dance last night?"

"Yes, I did."

"I didn't see you there."

"I just watched."

"Why didn't you dance. There were plenty of girls, weren't there?"

"With all of yesterday's preparations, I was really tired," he explains, inverting the last two words.

"It's difficult to get oriented on the first day. The dance in honor of Neptune is usually the most exciting of all, and it usually takes place when crossing the equator. You really must be baptized."

"Baptized? How?"

"Baptism consists of jumping into the pool in full costume. It's a lot of fun."

"I believe it."

"The movies are also good and for the most part haven't yet played in São Paulo. Are you from São Paulo?"

"Yes, I am. May I ask what you are reading, ma'am?" he asks, discarding some of his shyness.

"Miss," she corrects. "My name is Odete Ramos Penteado. I'm reading *The Devil's Advocate* by Morris West," her intonation reflects a dominant temperament. She can't be more than 25 years old.

"Are you enjoying it?"

"I'm only half-way through. Have you read it?"

"Yes."

"It describes Vatican politics quite well, don't you think?"

"Yes," he answers, startled. "That is, I think so," he corrects.

"The theme is quite gripping, and he seems to have a complete grasp of the subject."

"He's one of the best authors today."

"Have you read *The Process* by Franz Kafka?"

"I saw the film."

"The book is much superior. It shows the inconsistencies of human justice far better. The film hardly shows the scene of the young man with the woman of the 'easy life,' his roommate. She thinks that the police pursuit of him is because of some robbery or murder and takes him in without much hesitation. But when she finds out that the real reason for the persecution is political, she violently rejects him and moves out... I'm just prattling on, and that's not good for a girl who doesn't even know the name of the person she's talking to."

"I'm sorry, I should have mentioned it: Fernando Torres, or just Torres if you prefer."

"Torres, have you ever written anything?"

The words reverberate in his ears like a strange and beautiful melody. He has grown unaccustomed to feminine voices.

"I have only written some stories. How about you?"

"I am a modest poet with one small published book."

"Congratulations."

"Why?"

"To find your own book on the shelves of a bookstore must be both a reward and a satisfaction."

"Not really. Before it was published I used to think so. Afterwards, I discovered that this was also one of the illusions of life."

"Is life, then, so full of illusions?"

"I really don't know."

"As a poet I think you do. Is it not the poets who dream?" he asks, less inhibited. He was much more at ease.

44

"Dreaming is nothing more than a great illusion. Frequently, we dream of dreaming."

"Torres," interrupts Ruiz, "what a time I had finding you? Wasn't it supposed to be on the other side?"

"Yes, it was," he agrees, getting up and slowly recomposing himself from the shock.

A few moments pass with no-one saying a word. The young man speaks up to apologize.

"Allow me to introduce Miss Odete Ramos Penteado."

"Pleased to meet you. Alvaro Ruiz," he says, struggling not to show his surprise.

"Thank you," Odete responds, holding out her hand.

"Torres, the shops are still open," says the doctor, breaking another long and uncomfortable silence.

"Oh, yes, let's go. If you will excuse me, Odete."

"Of course, by all means."

"Well then, see you later."

"See you."

"What progress!" comments Ruiz as they walk toward the shops. "Were you the one who..."

"It was she."

"It's a good start. Did you find any good qualities?"

"She seems to be very nice."

"Don't make decisions on first impressions. Remember that we have to choose the ideal woman. Well, let's let it go for now," he says upon arriving at the shops.

The shops were quite varied. The articles on display had typical colors and aspects for Brazilian tastes. The prices, stamped in Liras, obliged the new tourists to make a complicated conversion to Brazilian currency.

They look in the shop windows and then go to the exchange cashier's window just beyond. Torres gets in line ahead of Ruiz.

"You won't have any expenses," intercepts the doctor.

"Why not? Aren't the clothes for me?"

"Of course! But, as the author of the test, all expenses are on me."

"But..."

"Don't argue. Case closed."

"Very well," he agrees with no more resistance. The money he has isn't really enough for these extravagances.

They buy three shirts, two pairs of shorts, two pairs of pants and a pair of Italian shoes. Torres feels in debt to Ruiz. Any indecision about the test, if it happens, will have to be abandoned. They go to the cabin to change clothes and then go to the pool.

The morning has warmed up and the south wind has eased off. The sea is like a Swiss lake. The pool is behind a high funnel, which is belching smoke and noise.

"How about that one over there?" suggests Ruiz, pointing out a young lady to his left.

"She's interesting."

"Just that...?"

"Well... I guess so."

"Cheer up, boy, you lack enthusiasm!"

"I'm sorry, I was a little distracted."

They end up seated on some benches on the side, the better to observe the activity of the swimmers. There are many for such a small pool. One has the feeling that the pool is frothing like a volcano.

"Did Odete make an impression on you?"

"I thought she was extremely nice."

"She's not very beautiful."

"But it's not only beauty that attracts," he corrects, defending her.

"I know, but it's a big help, isn't it?"

"Sometimes it just gets in the way."

"As a seminarian, you seem to be well versed in the subject!"

Torres doesn't respond and lowers his head.

"Did I hurt your feelings?"

"No."

"See that blonde up ahead, there?" indicates the doctor as a means of apology. "She's fairly attractive, don't you think?"

"Quite."

"She must be a foreigner. What do you think about getting to know a foreigner?"

"It might be interesting."

"On second thought, I think we should avoid them because of language difficulties. There are plenty of Brazilian girls to choose from," says Ruiz, showing a certain enthusiasm. "Do you know how to approach a girl?"

"I don't understand."

"I asked if you know how to make contact, talk to a girl."

"I don't think so."

"The first moment of contact is one of the most difficult and one of the most important phases, so you must take great care. You approach the girl slowly, looking to both sides, you can even whistle. But you mustn't show any interest whatever. It is essential that you seem to be there casually.

Let a few moments go by, then look at her and say: 'A fairly hot day, don't you think?' Be sure to check the weather conditions beforehand. You could also say, 'It's so windy on the high seas, isn't it?' This kind of dialog gives excellent results. Do you get it?"

"Yes."

"Then, depending on the girl's reaction, you might change the subject, and there you are."

"Instead of talking about the weather, wouldn't it be better to simply say: Italy?" Torres suggests.

"Why?" Ruiz asks, intrigued.

"One asks if the girl's destination is Italy. The ideal of the voyage is linked to our person which induces sympathy."

"You surprise me. Where did you learn that?"

"Odete."

"You're being taken in by that young lady, and that could hurt the test. Let's look for some others to meet. It would be quite a coincidence if the first contact were the ideal."

Blondes, brunettes and redheads pass by. Some quite nice, others not so.

Torres feels he is being frivolous. Perhaps the fear of seeing himself obliged to talk with a woman is part of the reason. He is ill at ease, he squirms about continuously, and he wishes he were far away from there.

...I discovered later that this was also one of the illusions of life, he remembers from one of his moments with Odete. With her, the problem is already resolved: a simple *hello* would be enough.

His thoughts stick to Odete and obliterate the virtues of the other girls. He wants to explore that disillusion. A poet, intelligent and nice are difficult virtues to find.

The doctor struggles to stir up some interest. But it's impossible to overcome Torres' apathy. When they agree on the beauty of some young girl, Torres refuses to act, alleging some supposed inner frivolity.

After a while they give up the search and, overcoming the reluctance of the younger man, they both dive into the crowded pool. Their bodies, heated by the sun, are delightfully cooled off by the cold saltwater which is constantly being replaced by the pumps.

Ruiz leaves the pool shortly and goes to the bar, looking for cigarettes. Torres gets out of the water and sits on one of the benches next to some other swimmers.

"Hello!" calls out a feminine voice.

Startled, he turns around, unsure if he is the one being addressed.

"Odete!" he exclaims, surprised, getting up at the same time.

"Are you trying to get your bearings?"

"Oh, yes. Let's sit down on that bench over there," he says, pointing at a vacant space just ahead.

"Did you like the water?"

"Very much. Have you been here long?"

"Yes."

"How is it that I didn't see you?"

"I was just behind you and that gentleman. What were you looking for? I saw you pointing at some girls, and then it looked like you had given up on something."

"Pointing? It was nothing; we were just observing."

"Is it a secret?"

"Well... a kind of prank."

"That man is rather strange... Is he a relative?"

"I met him on this voyage. We are sharing the same cabin."

"I have the impression that he's a girl chaser."

"That's just an impression. He... oh, never mind."

"You two were up to something, weren't you?"

Embarrassed, Torres laughs, demonstrating just why women find him charming.

She continues to exude her contagious tranquillity. Her well-formed body has on a bikini and her damp hair falls about her shoulders. Her nearly naked condition is strange to the young man.

"I don't know, yet."

"You're pretty undecided for a single guy surrounded by so many girls!"

"Are there really that many?"

"Haven't you become aware of all the looks you've been getting? You're being noticed!"

"Why?" he asks, surprised.

"Well, it's just that you're one of the few men available."

"Oh, I see..."

"Shall we take a walk?"

He agrees and they start walking around on the deck. He is slightly taller than she. Torres walks cautiously. He feels a strange physical attraction for her coming over him. These reactions, nipped in the bud until now, now require perfect self-control of him.

"Are you enjoying the voyage?"

"Very much so," he answers, continuing to look straight ahead. He is afraid to look at her.

"Am I upsetting you?"

"Absolutely not."

At her suggestion, they go to the deck bar which is crawling with people at that hour. Odete waits for him to offer her a cocktail. Minutes go by in small talk.

"Aren't you going to drink something?" she prompts.

"Yes, let's have something. What would you like?" he asks quickly.

"A dry martini."

"I'll have one, too," he confirms with relief. He doesn't know the names of any cocktails.

"*Camariere, due martini!*", she says to the steward.

"You speak Italian?"

"Just a little, from my first voyage."

"Have you been to other countries besides Italy?"

"All of Europe."

"That's a lot, isn't it? I always wanted to travel and get to know other countries."

"Why don't you travel more often?"

"It's impossible, practically impossible."

"Financial problems?"

"I would say so."

"What is your profession, then?"

"I'm... a teacher."

"A teacher of what?"

"Philosophy," he answers with some relief. "I would like to hear some of your poems."

She thinks for a moment. She wants to ask why the sudden change of subject, but decides not to and resolves to satisfy his request.

"I once loved a bird
that flew away, taking my hopes with him.
He flew, around the world he flew, and then returned.
He perched upon my shoulder
And spoke of adventures and desires.
He loved me, but I no longer loved him.
I once loved a bird…"

"That's one of my poems."

"Is it in your book?"

"No, I made it up at the pool," she says.

"Frustrated love?"

"No."

"Nothing happens without a reason."

"Perhaps I am afraid to love," she replies, pensive.

"You are that afraid of love?" he exclaims with an odd naturalness.

"Man is afraid to love nature and goes blind. He is afraid to love music and goes deaf. He is afraid to love and is scorned."

"Strange, very strange," he says, not a little surprised.

"Why strange? Life is one eternal fear: the poor of being sick, and rich of being poor; youth of becoming old, and the old of dying. To fear is life, and life is to fear," she adds, laughing.

The waiter brings the martinis. She toasts him with a gesture of familiarity. Torres, however, doesn't even know how to hold the glass. He is one step behind her in everything.

"Tell me something about yourself," he asks, breaking the silence.

"I studied social science, I live alone with my mother, my father abandoned us, and that's it. This afternoon there's a good film showing."

"Which one?"

"Jean Harlow in *Platinum Venus*. Are you going to see it?"

"Yes. May I invite you?"

"I think it was I who just invited you! At 3:00 p.m. on the command bridge. Now, if you'll excuse me, I'm going to the hairdresser," she says as she gets up.

They say good-bye. The number of swimmers at the bar has diminished considerably. He sits back down, his fingers twirling the glass on the table, his eyes fixed upon it, and his mind wanders in thought. Only a short time ago, he had only one aim in life, and all his inspirations and all the strength of his affections ran in a single direction. Now strange sensations direct his thoughts and his efforts to a greater destiny. His life was no longer a single unit, coherent in itself.

He finishes the martini, pays, and walks with his head lowered toward the cabin. A hot shower doesn't manage to divert his spirit.

...you're afraid to test yourself; if, in fact, your faith is solid as a rock, nothing can upset it. But, if you run away from the fight, how can you know the degree of that faith?

Ruiz is right: first, the doubt; then, the certainty.

A gong sounds from the loudspeaker.

"All passengers: the second meal, first sitting, is served."

Torres leaves the cabin, encounters a few hurrying passengers, and arrives at the dining salon. The doctor is already seated at their table, waiting for him.

They begin to talk about nothing in particular. Ruiz deliberately says nothing about the test. He acts as though nothing is happening.

The waiter serves them lentil soup; wine and bread accompany this first dish.

"It's time for you to resume the story of your past," says the doctor.

"Do you really think it's necessary? I only wanted to amuse you, remember?"

"Now I really must insist on the rest. I want to know everything about your personality. It's a long voyage and we will have, or rather I think we will have, time to talk about your life," he says, winking cynically.

The young man isn't quite sure of the meaning of the wink.

"Do you have anything on for this afternoon?"

"I'm going with Odete to the movies."

"I see. Permit me, however, to make a slight correction. One doesn't say, 'I'm going with Odete to the movies...' Take charge of her and say, 'Odete is going with me to the movies!' And one other thing: you're letting yourself be taken in by this girl. It's necessary that we find some others to meet," he insists.

"You really think it absolutely necessary?"

"Without a doubt. Tomorrow we start over again with the conquests. Agreed?"

"Very well."

"I think I may be losing my companion for the voyage. Although we could play a few games of chess."

"But we can always play a few games..."

"There won't be time, I'm sure. Well, I think you can get on with the story of your past."

The waiter serves the dessert.

Chapter IV

At 14, Torres was in the ninth grade. Insofar as he was concerned, he had complete freedom. His bicycle took him everywhere, and swimming, fishing, sneaking up on lovers at night in the park and scaring them, puppet theaters and movies made up his day with no time left over for studying.

Studying... well, studying was for sissies. He just couldn't fit it into his life. He was tempted to quit school and focus his attention on any profitable venture. So he was like a bird set free, hard to capture. The table, piled high with books and notepads, repelled him.

Like a good son, he had put into practice his mother's advice: "Fernando, enjoy your childhood, because it's the best time of your life, and study as well."

Quick on the uptake as a child, he concluded that the verb 'study' had nothing to do with the first part of the advice. Much to his mother's unhappiness, he wasn't interested in the building blocks of education. He explored all the childish and juvenile emotions with intensity.

Silvia, the clever destroyer of priestly vocations, had moved far away and no longer held the slightest influence over him.

During this time, he became, just like his playmates, quite shy around girls. The school principal was the main cause behind this generalized reserve. This gentleman had ordered that a line be drawn in the school yard separating the sexes. Girls on one side and boys on the other. They were, therefore, beings of a pathetic heterogeneity.

You couldn't even talk to the girls close to the school. Between classes, long and furtive glances were exchanged across the line. These glances, quick at first, nearly always stopped at the line, fearful of some reprimand. In moments of daring, the boys had the urge to run up to the line, stamp on it and hurl themselves, breathlessly, into the arms of the girls. The movies at that time favored such fantasies.

* * *

"Since contact was forbidden at school, you took that fear, unconsciously, into everyday life," adds Ruiz. "Perhaps that was the reason behind the general timidity. Principals, as a general rule, lack preparation for the position, and that deficiency is reflected in the moral education they give the students since they represent the first civil authority encountered by young people. Go on."

* * *

Girls were, then, partially removed from his life. If, at that time, some priestly inspiration should happen to occur, it would fall on fertile ground.

He was, for certain, like Rousseau's Emile. Contact with the fields and the underbrush at the fishing holes revealed to him, just like the character in Rousseau, the science of living. He refused to be, by studying, a data file. This negative education would overload his memory, eliminating all spontaneity from him.

* * *

"How I would have liked to have lived your childhood in the interior, in Botucatu. My childhood was asphyxiated in São Paulo. I have no recollections of the sound and beauty of the fields to cheer me up when I need it. Well, we're getting off the subject. What was your professional inclination at that time?"

* * *

The ninth grade final exams were coming to an end. Torres had already been held back in two subjects for a makeup term: Portuguese – a subject in which he managed to quite easily make 36 mistakes in a single paper – and mathematics – he had studied 62 theorems in a single night, discarding two as being unworkable. But they were workable.

Only the science exam remained. He simply couldn't afford another failing grade because the limit for a makeup term was two subjects. If he didn't get at least a minimum passing grade, he would fail the year, which mattered little to him but was important to his parents. His father was quite strict. Torres feared some violent and vexing action that might keep him from sitting down for some time. There was nothing to do but study with a will. He studied. He borrowed notebooks – because he didn't have any – from more efficient classmates and sacrificed an hour for three days running. This nearly wore him out.

Science at that time consisted of the concepts of the general scientific culture. Among the theories taught were 'Darwin and the Origin of the Species' and 'Freud and Psychoanalysis.'

"Man descended from the apes," said his notebook. Nobody would ever convince him that Darwin was not an excessively hairy man, of crude and brutal features. He identified him with the gorillas of the Tarzan films, except that he wore clothes. He could even feel the hot breath from his wide nostrils.

"...and the small apes? I guess they became dwarfs. Maybe that's why we, men of all sizes, like bananas!" he exclaimed, satisfactorily convinced.

"And Adam and Eve?"

I no longer understood anything, but it didn't matter. I was satisfied to know that man had descended from monkeys, and as for the rest of the subject I would elaborate on physical resemblance, taste for bananas, etc. He went on to another thesis.

"Freud and Psychoanalysis;" he perked up a little more on this theme. "The studies of Freud are closely related to hypnosis," said the notebook.

The previous year a professor, who was called Professor for no apparent reason, and who hypnotized, had come to Botucatu. In one of his sessions at the Cassino Cinema, Torres, curious as a monkey, went on stage with five other persons. The man with distinctive features and unusually wide-open eyes frightened him. Fearfully, he held back behind the others as unfortunate as himself. Everyone was trying to hide behind everyone else.

"Halt," ordered the Professor.

They halted.

"Form a line in front of me."

They formed into a ragged line.

"Form up this way," he corrected, taking them by their arms and placing them in the correct position.

His voice, with a noticeable accent, exuded mystery.

"Now, don't be afraid," he said to the six, who had already shrunk back two steps.

"Be calm! Now look into my eyes."

Torres didn't want to look. The man was the devil himself, come straight from the fires of hell without his trident.

"Your eyelids are becoming heavy, very heavy, even more heavy. When I tell you to close them, they will close."

"Close!" he barked in a commanding voice.

They closed.

"You no longer have a will of your own; you will obey my every command. Now then, play a piano concert."

Torres began to move his fingers in the air as if they were playing the keys of a piano.

The audience roared with laughter. His companions performed feats worthy of virtuosos. The applause encouraged them. Their fingers opened up and their arms crossed gracefully.

"Stop!" ordered the Professor.

They stopped. Their arms fell to their sides, their eyes closed.

"Who are you?" he asked Torres randomly.

"Rubinstein," he responded. It was not a common name for him.

After talking to each of the others, he ordered them to take up a baton and conduct a symphony orchestra.

Torres' first reaction was to run his hand through his hair and mess it up. He extended his arms, waited briefly, and began to conduct the 'orchestra.' Once again, it was the movies which had shown him the way to behave like a musical performer. His expression, as he learned later, was constricted, showing great concentration. He could even hear the musical instruments.

"Stop!"

"Who are you?"

"Toscanini," he answered, proudly.

Fortunately, that was the end of his pathetic performance. He stumbled down the steps and sat down in his place, somewhat confused. A few still remained on the stage. A young lady, as she had been commanded, returned to her childhood. Her voice, her gestures and the rocking of imaginary dolls were characteristic of her age. A man went into a cataleptic state, looking almost dead.

Freud, like the Professor, had also hypnotized him. Torres was seduced by the mystery that emanated from him. He forgot that he was studying and went on to the next annotation.

Hypnosis was used as a means for healing. He brought a hysterical woman back to her senses by exploring the mental past of the patient. This case is known as 'The Case of Anna O.,' he read.

Newton's Law was applied to scientific ideas of the time. He stopped reading, turned back the pages and re-read the previous ideas.

Rubinstein, Toscanini.

No worldly power would ever separate the figure of Freud from that of the Professor who had hypnotized him. Later he would confirm from photographs that the penetrating look on their faces was the same.

For the next few days, he was overwhelmed by the doctrine of Sigmund Freud. An unworldly force emanated from him, his posture straightened, and his chest projected forward.

I don't know why I can't hypnotize my little sister; I open my eyes so wide! he thought at the time.

"I almost forgot. I did pass the science exam", interjects Torres.

During the exam the examiner, an educated man with a kind heart, was devastated by the scientific ignorance of the boy. Tired of asking questions that were not answered, he asked him about what he already knew. Darwin, and especially Freud, were responsible for his not being held back for another year in the ninth grade.

* * *

"If these two wise men had not existed, where would you be now?!" interrupts Ruiz. "The work of these scientists rewarded you with promotion," he concludes with a smile.

* * *

The following day he sought out the teacher and questioned him insistently about psychoanalysis. The teacher patiently told him of the circumstances of Freud's Viennese experience.

"Freud," he said, "was enthusisticall dedicated to the psychological treatment of neurotics. He made a series of discoveries that culminated in the elaboration of psychoanalysis."

"Just what is psychoanalysis?"

"It's a special method for exploring the subconscious by means of psychological analysis."

"And what is psychological analysis?"

What is psychological analysis? Torres had transformed himself into a consummate 'questioner.'

The teacher was patient.

"The Psychoanalist observes and analyzes the facts of the intellect, or better, of the soul, determining its causes and precepts."

The movies in that era were rich in scenes of relclining couches that received bodies that had pathogenic minds. Artists resorted constantly to the couch. Any little thing and there they were in a hurry lying down.

Torres was preoccupied with the idea of receiving patients, leading them to the couch and hypnotizing them with airs of untouchable wisdom. This scene was the center of his imagination from his 15th to his 17th year.

* * *

"Did you actually try do something about this, or did you merely have dreams of curing emotional disturbances," asks Ruiz.

* * *

During these two years he searched the past of many people to feed his imagination. His greatest enthusiasm consisted of discovering the inclinations of several of his teachers. Every teacher has a penchant, sometimes unknown to himself, for certain topics of his own subject matter.

In class, he concentrated on checking the tone of voice, physical appearance and repetitions of subject matter: these cinematic reactions showed him the proclivities of his teachers. Before exams and weekly reviews, he asked questions of previous years students in the upper grades; this always produced excellent results.

In history, he accomplished one of his greatest exploits. He wanted to know if a personality was good or bad; everything else he could pick up at random. The disposition of the bad guys or the good guys in the past were always the same. He filled up six or seven pages on this subject within an hour. Pity the poor teacher so flooded by the great number of pages!

It would be good to mention here that this astuteness helped him considerably in making up cheat sheets. If it hadn't been for the cheat sheets, he would still be studying today. Now he consoled himself with Rousseau; he didn't need to be a data file full of interpretations.

* * *

"I also used these devices," confesses Ruiz. "A lot of years have gone by, but I remember how it was. At that time, languages were dreadful! In the end, why did you give up psychiatry?"

* * *

When Torres was 17, he came up against serious obstacles to his psychiatric pretensions. He couldn't stand biology. What a tiresome and futile subject! The cheat sheets started being used by the time of the second review session. At first, because he knew of the necessity of the subject for the medical entrance exams, he was assiduous. But he grew apathetic with it and, to soothe his conscience, he resolved to make new efforts to apply himself to the science of living beings.

On Christmas day of that year, he had lunch at home with a psychiatrist.

* * *

"That day was one of those crossroads that you referred to," says the young man.

* * *

This doctor, a civil servant from the town of Juqueri, took his Freudian pretensions, crushed them, threw them on the ground and spit on them. His disillusion was complete and irreversible. What awaited him, he discovered, was intense study, a future of dealing with 'total nut cases' in public insane asylums and an accumulation of material discomfiture due to a low salary.

* * *

Ruiz settles himself in the chair. He knows that this attack is not aimed at him, but he can feel the feathers of the arrow as it goes by.

"Fortunately, the influence of American movies and books have given new life to this troubled profession. The 'American way of life' made a visit to the psychoanalyst a comforting and regular procedure. You had your inspiration a few years too soon," says Ruiz. "Well, let's stop for now; you can continue your story at dinner."

Lunch was over. Chairs were scraped back, and the buzzing that comes from well fed people filled the atmosphere.

Chapter V

Lunch over, they return to their cabin. Torres takes off his shoes and climbs up into his berth. He lies down, face turned toward the porthole. The sea is calm and the sky cloudless. There's not a living soul to be seen in all that vastness.

His eyes fix on the line where the sky meets the sea, and it takes some effort to keep them open. He feels that God is observing that same point. Suddenly, a desire for close contact with Him springs up within him. Religion is too deeply rooted to allow a separation longer than a day, and he acknowledges that he is one of His disciples in the plenitude of his soul.

A happy memory of the seminary infuses the pleasure that he is enjoying. There is nothing, he is now quite sure, that can supplant the happiness that he has known, and he experiences a deep yearning. At the height of his emotion, he prays with growing and uncontrollable faith. His heavy breathing reveals the feelings that have control of him.

His conscience is at ease insofar as the results of the test are concerned; the experiment can neither harm the beliefs of his religion nor would it ever. But the lack of worship is suffocating him. Ruiz was right to ask him to abandon the daily mass. Only in this manner could the test take place under nearly equal terms.

He continues praying and meditating, until he remembers his date with Odete. Startled, he looks at his watch. It is already 3 o'clock. Hurriedly, he gets down from his berth, and, putting on his shoes, he awakens his companion.

"Where are you going in such a hurry?" he asks, stretching.

"I'm late for the date."

"You managed to be late!" he exclaims with surprise.

The young man does not answer. His distraction was unintentional and caused by his concern for the weather.

"See you later," he says as he leaves, slamming the door behind him.

He runs up the stairs and arrives breathless at the lounge. Odete is waiting.

"How times have changed. It used to be that it was the man who had to wait. Ten minutes!"

"I'm sorry. My being late is really unforgivable."

"I don't think we need to make a scene out it," she adds, smiling.

She seems more beautiful The sleeveless print dress clings to her body with femininity. Her well-combed hair and facial makeup blend together coquettishly. Odete continues to radiate her magnetic amiability.

Torres finds himself slightly distracted and ill at ease, and can't adjust to the situation. The enchantment of that afternoon together and his sudden rush up the stairs have clouded his mind.

"The film must have already begun," she says, noticing the indecision of her friend.

"Oh, yes! The movie."

"What deep meditations are you having?"

"Was I meditating? I really don't know, I guess…"

"If my company is undesirable, I can let you go, if that's what you want," she interrupts, somewhat irritated.

"Oh, no," he amends quickly, "not at all."

"Shall we go in, then?"

"Couldn't we go later? I would like to take a stroll on deck."

"I don't know if you've noticed, but this is the first time you've expressed a desire. I was about to give up."

"Give up on what?"

"Of hearing you make a request!"

They go up the stairs. The deck is nearly deserted. They sit in two lounge chairs facing the ocean. Some people are reading, others talk out of earshot, and the waves crashing against the hull create a monotonous deep rumble.

"Forgive my indiscretion. This morning I had the impression that you were awakening to life; it was as though you had been isolated like a sick person for a long period and then had suddenly recovered your health.

"I don't know how to explain it to you; I am shy by nature, and I take a long time to get used to people."

"Is it only shyness, or has some romantic disillusionment made you put off women?"

"Romantic disillusionment! Oh! Well, I did suffer an infatuation, but it didn't work out. Maybe my shyness stems from that."

"Well, I thought it might be something like that!…"

Torres had never lied so much in his life.

"Are you traveling alone?"

"No, my mother is with me. Why?"

"Just curiosity."

"If you keep on with these mysterious ways, I think I shall leave you alone. Don't you ever come down to earth?"

"I'm trying."

"Why don't you tell me about the affair? It might help..."

"Help how, Odete? And what affair?"

"Well, I just don't know what to think... Your frustrated love affair. Isn't that the reason you are standoffish?"

"Ah! My affair. Yes, of course, I shall tell you."

"Then get on with it," she says, becoming somewhat annoyed.

"Are you really that upset?"

"No," she answers with a smile, "but do get on with it."

"My affair... no, you'd better tell me about your affairs, and then I'll tell you about mine."

"My affairs?! But I haven't had any!" she exclaims, upset.

"You haven't? But everybody has. Tell me yours first," he asks insistently.

"As far as I can tell, my affair is just starting," she whispers.

"What did you say?"

"Nothing. Let's talk about something specific. We look like a couple of fools."

"I agree."

"Let's begin with me, then. I was ten years old when my father left us. Mother suffered a great deal, and I missed him a lot as well. We were quite well off because he left us with a good monthly income. But his absence couldn't be compensated quite so easily.

"I'm very sorry..."

"Well, life isn't perfect. Mother, not having anyone to cling to, turned all her attention to me. She raised me with exaggerated caution and was always alerting me to the dangers of marriage. The few flirtations and boyfriends that I had were rejected by her at first sight, and I always wound up agreeing with her.

"I turned to poetry," she went on, "because I could vent all my accumulated feelings in it. My classmates were getting married. I rebuffed some other amorous attempts, and time rolled on... A short time ago, I realized that the blame for these misfortunes was not entirely hers. My mother's bitterness symbolized for me, perhaps unconsciously, what marriage was about. I was afraid of going through what she had."

Suddenly, Torres is aware of the harm that he may have caused. He has acted completely selfishly up to that moment, thinking that the test was meant to awaken love in him alone. He had not thought about the reciprocity of that affection. How could he keep up this farce without knowing its outcome? He had wanted to put his vocation to the test and had accepted the test because he had had some moments of depression while at the seminary. On those occasions, he had envied the spontaneity of a father-son relationship and had also felt the need to share secrets with a woman, a woman who was his wife.

The knowledge of secret loves and the disturbances of the soul that he would be privy to in the confessional would aggravate those doubts. In the future, he would be able to use Odete as a shield against the uncertainties of the spirit. Between service to God and love, which would lay claim to his soul? The answer would necessarily be known by the end of the voyage, but the fact of having created it would turn all his plans to ashes. Odete should not be harmed by the outcome of an egotistical drama.

"I think that for your own good we shouldn't meet anymore," he interrupts.

"Is it because of your love affair?"

"Yes, that's right. I am taking this trip to forget her. When you saw me at the pool with Ruiz, we were looking for a girl whose purpose would be... well, you can imagine."

"No, go on."

"We were looking for a girl... well, just that."

"I understand what you're trying to say. And if I take the risk, perhaps I could use you for a similar purpose. You might make my mother and I change our concept of marriage. Now, wait a minute, we're getting a little carried away. This is all very interesting; we've only met a short while ago and already we are apologizing to each other."

"Then, we may be able to help each other!"

"Like good friends," she adds.

"Like good friends," he agrees, relieved. "I would like to read your book of poetry."

"Do you like poetry?"

"I really don't know. Some poetry, like modern art, requires profound study. I think that everything that goes against simplicity and clarity hurts its own authenticity."

"I agree with you, and I can add that everything in life is a reflection of struggle: the poor struggle against the rich; the rich the even richer; the ignoramus the educated; the educated the even more educated. This desire to be more than someone else is translated frequently in literature and in rhetoric, searching for proper terms.

"Then recite one of your poems."

> *"Yesterday there was the uncertain, hope.*
> *Today there is reality, happening.*
> *Tomorrow there will be uncertainty, disillusion."*

70

"Disillusion never leaves you," he observes.

"There isn't all that much disillusion."

Every once in a while Torres is surprised to find himself analyzing her characteristics. Her sweet smile reflects the purity of her soul and feelings. He is astonished that she has never married. Her congeniality put to the test her suitors' task. What defects could be found by her mother? Could this reaction be a kind of excuse for being abandoned? It's difficult to answer for one who doesn't have imperfections! Human nature itself is imperfect. After all, man is subject to the suffering caused by the seven deadly sins, and it's easier to accept defects and try to correct them than to extirpate them like a malignant cancer. That must be the key to modern psychology.

The unusual silence continues to foster obscure meditations. Odete confirms, in this moment of retreat, the impression that Torres had made on her from the first moment she saw him. The peace that comes over him fascinates her. She feels comfortable at his side. She recognizes with complete candor that there is an enormous difference between him and the boys she has known.

"You're quite mysterious."

"Not really."

"A few days from now, when our friendship has become cemented, I'm going to ask a favor of you."

"What's that?"

"I want to introduce you to my mother to see what defect she can find in you."

"Now, Odete, don't get ahead of yourself. You don't know me that well, yet."

"It's not necessary. When a person is, he is; when he's not, he's not. I don't know where I read that."

"Despite your adage, I think that only time will reveal our weaknesses. Often they're so deeply embedded that their appearance takes years."

"Have you ever heard of feminine intuition?"

"Yes, and I've heard of its failures just as often."

"How do you know there are so many like that" she asks, wondering.

Study at the seminary analyzed the most intricate human problems. He remembered some examples and wanted to tell them, but he was afraid of revealing his identity.

"Well... around, relatives, friends..."

"But that's not good enough. You're hiding a big secret and don't want to reveal it to me. That's not fair of you, because I told you all about my life and you won't tell about yours."

"Let's leave it for later. Do you think the second showing has begun? I'm really interested in that film."

"Without a doubt you are a terrible liar. Your face has turned red, accusing you."

"I've turned red?"

"And how! You look like a stop light. That's the third time today!"

"Shall we go, then?" he asks awkwardly.

"As you like."

The film is dubbed in Italian. Torres understands almost nothing, and from time to time asks Odete for an explanation. She translates some of his requests and others on her own volition.

The girl follows the film with great interest, giving the impression that she is living the scenes. At the end, when Jean Harlow dies of pneumonia, she stops translating and becomes completely absorbed. Her quick fingers dab away a tear at the corner of her eye.

The lights go up. The cinema is a semi-circular amphitheater and holds about three hundred people.

As they walk along the long corridors of the ship, the gong of the loudspeaker sounds: "Attention all passengers, the first sitting for dinner is now being served."

"Are you in the first sitting?" she asks.

"Yes."

"Hurry up, then. They don't like it when we're late."

"I'll go straight there," he says and at the same time says his good-byes.

"Wait a minute. Are we going to the dance tonight?"

"Yes. Where shall I meet you?" he says, turning around to face her.

"I'll wait for you in my cabin. It's three doors down from yours."

"How did you know… I mean, did you see me go in?" he asks, distressed.

Is it possible she saw me in a cassock or my clerical suit? he thinks.

"Don't be so upset. I saw you go in yesterday afternoon. Why are you blushing again?"

Torres laughs, relieved, and tries to hide his alarm a little.

"Well then, I'll see you later." He says, hurrying away.

He arrives, panting, trembling a little from his recent scare and finds the doctor waiting for him.

Was she telling the truth?

Ruiz pours wine into the glasses. The younger man is still breathing heavily and, because of that, takes a long drink of wine. He grasps the bottle, fills his glass again, and drinks nearly half of it.

"Ah! That's better!" he says, relieved. "What a scare I had!"

"Were you with that Odete?"

"Yes."

"I have a surprise for you."

Torres doesn't show any interest. He picks up a piece of bread and swallows three large spoons of soup; he wants to line his stomach. The amount and the rapidity with which he had drunk the wine was already beginning to take effect.

"Don't you want to know?"

"Of course. Tell me."

"This afternoon I met a couple who are friends of mine. They have a daughter who is a raving beauty and very nice. I think you ought to meet her."

"Another?!"

"What do you mean, another? You seem to be tiring very quickly. Remember what we agreed on?"

"No, I don't."

"The deal was that you would find some girls and try to compare them. Otherwise, the test could be contaminated."

The waiter serves them roast goat, potatoes, peas and asparagus.

Torres eats, paying little attention to what he is doing. His mind shifts back and forth between Ruiz and Odete.

"All right, I agreed with your initial plan and I can't dodge it now. But I think it is unnecessary, totally unnecessary. Odete is right for the part."

"Possibly so, but we have to compare her. Do you have a date with her tonight?"

"I'm supposed to pick her up at ten o'clock for the dance. Until then I have nothing else to do."

"Very well, I set up a meeting for eight o'clock with Rosely's parents and another gentleman to play bridge. You will be able to talk to their daughter in the sitting room."

"Can't we leave it for tomorrow? Odete might see and…"

"She won't see. Most certainly she will be getting dressed for the dance."

Dessert arrives. The taste of the cheese cannot be covered up by the horrible coffee. They take their last sip of wine and get up satisfied. The flask is a little more emptier with each meal.

* * *

"Torres, I'd like to introduce you to Rosely Gonçalves de Almeida."

"I'm pleased to meet you. I'm Fernando Torres."

"Pleased to meet you," she says.

The young woman is exactly as Ruiz had described her. She is slightly shorter than he, and her thin, erect figure reminds him of a model. Her age is somewhere between 24 and 26.

"If you'll excuse me, my bridge partners are waiting," apologizes Ruiz, leaving the room.

The two of them remain frozen in place, facing each other. The young man, not knowing what else to do, invites her to sit down.

Torres can't take his focus off the girl's green eyes. It's as if he were hypnotized; she is truly beautiful.

"Are you going to Europe for a vacation?" he asks, a little disconcerted.

"Yes," she answers, coolly.

"For how long?" He doesn't know what to say, and his hands break out in a cold sweat.

"Three to four months," She is not helping him. She gives the impression of being forced to be there.

The sitting room is rapidly filling up. Chess and checkers tables, armchairs and a few ordinary chairs are being occupied. The tone of the voices as well as the smiles upon their faces shows the gaiety of the passengers.

"Are you going to the dance, tonight?" asks Rosely, breaking the uncomfortable silence. The other voices drown out hers.

"What? I can't hear you too well."

"I asked if you are going to the dance, tonight," she repeats a little louder.

"To the dance? Well, I don't know, yet. Perhaps I will."

"It should be very nice. Pity it's full dress."

"Is it full dress?"

"Didn't you know? It's the gala departure dance."

"Now what? What am I going to do? I don't have tuxedo!"

"Are you going?" she asks, again.

"I don't know. I haven't gone dancing, lately."

"Why?" she asks, surprised.

"I've been sick... that is, I had my appendix out."

"What a shame! There are so few boys..."

"But I saw a lot," he adds, trying to console her. In his innocence, he doesn't realize what a gaffe he has made.

She goes silent. She has taken his answer to be a snub. She is used to being treated with nicety. She is well aware of her physical endowments. His indifference can only be justified by interest in another girl. She is hurt and seeks retribution.

"I know there are many other boys. I'm with a very good group," she affirms, proudly, satisfied with her defense.

"Oh, good. Then you will be able to go with them," he declares, clumsily.

What brutish disinterest! she thinks, angrily. *Who does he think he is? If he thinks I'm offering myself, he's greatly mistaken!*

"If you will excuse me, I must get dressed for the dance," she says.

"Of course," he agrees, relieved. "As you wish."

"See you later."

Torres smiles politely, and she doesn't even open her mouth. She turns her back and strides out.

It doesn't do any good to insist, he thinks, defending himself to Ruiz, *the test has to be made with Odete. The dance!* he suddenly remembers, and, leaving the room, he begins to walk about aimlessly. Desperate, he goes to the bar and orders a martini – it's the only drink he knows. *I'll have to find her, now. I can't let her get dressed. What excuse can I offer?*

He gulps down the drink. The liquid burns his throat; he gags. He gets up, pays for the drink, and leaves hurriedly.

Before losing courage, he heads swiftly toward Odete's cabin. He passes by his own, stops a moment to catch his breath, and counts three doors ahead. He knocks. An older woman answers.

"Is Odete here?" he asks, nervously.

"Yes, she is," she answers, looking him up and down.

The woman continues to look at him as though waiting for something. Her manner embarrasses him.

"Did you wish to speak to her?"

"Yes, please, only for a minute," he apologizes, hoping to win her over.

"I can't invite you in because she is getting dressed. Please excuse me," she says with some asperity.

This animosity washes over him. The words he had rehearsed are stuck in his mind.

"Oh, it's you!" says the girl, closing the door behind her.

A beautiful red ball gown covers her figure. Her disheveled hair shows that she was combing it out.

"Odete... I don't even know how to say it, but I can't go to the dance."

"You can't? But why?" she asks, surprised.

"Well... I had an operation shortly before the voyage. I had my appendix out," stumbling over his words and mixing up everything.

"Has it been very long since your operation?"

"About a month."

"Then it won't harm you."

"Yes, it will... I also didn't pack a tuxedo; I wasn't thinking about dancing because of the operation, and I didn't bring a tuxedo," he repeats.

Undeniably he is a terrible liar.

"You're blushing, again."

"Me? I think it must be the afternoon sun, don't you?"

"Quite likely!" she responds cynically.

Torres, tangled up in all the lies he has told, hangs his head, waiting for some reproach.

"And just what will we do if you don't want to go out?"

"We can talk in the glass enclosed part of the deck."

"All right. I'll go change my clothes, then," she says, going back in and closing the door with a smile.

"She can even be most considerate. I think she accepted my excuses," he sighs, relieved.

Five minutes later, she reappears wearing slacks and a sweater.

"Let's go."

"Yes, let's. You're not angry?"

"About the dance?"

"Yes, you were so anxious to go!"

"The dance was just an excuse to have fun with my good friend," she says, stressing the last two words.

At midnight, after the *Sandwich Service* in the Day Room, he takes her to her cabin. They say good bye smiling, their happiness is a reflection of the pleasant night they have spent together.

Torres, entering his cabin, finds Ruiz waiting for him.

"I've been thinking and I have come to the conclusion that I ought to know everything that is going on; that's the only way I'll be able to help later on. Don't you agree?"

"I don't see any objection to that."

"Then start talking. Before that, however, change into pajamas and get in bed. Now."

Two hours later, sleep overcomes them.

* * *

On the following day, the young man arrives at lunch before his friend. Wine is served and he tells the grumbling waiter that he will wait for Ruiz. The Italian ponders the delay. The second sitting should begin 45 minutes after the start of the first.

Ruiz appears 15 minutes later. He apologizes profusely to the waiter without effect. He continues mumbling and his gesticulations cause others to stare. A healthy tip from the doctor, placed on the table, is enough to stem the verbal hemorrhage of the man. He smiles and gently serves them their soup.

"I was with Rosely," says Ruiz.

"The girl from last night?"

"Yes, she's quite upset with you. I think you owe her an apology. After all, just what was your impression of her?"

"I'm absolutely convinced that the test should be made with Odete."

"Are you sure about that? The other one is much prettier, isn't she?"

"Possibly, but she has neither the sweetness nor the simplicity of Odete..."

"Before I forget," he adds, "Rosely asked me to tell you she wants to talk to you after lunch, without fail."

"But I can't. I have a date at three o'clock."

"Look for her at two o'clock; her cabin is in the same corridor, no. 1044."

After coffee, they separate once again.

At two o'clock, Torres knocks on the door at 1044. The girl must have been waiting for him because she opens it immediately.

"Good afternoon. Dr. Ruiz told me you wished to speak with me," he explains awkwardly.

"That's right. Wait a few minutes, and I'll walk out with you," she offers, quite aware that it is not an invitation. "I think we owe each other a mutual apology for last night. I don't want you to have a bad impression of me," says the girl, walking with him to the bridge.

It all seems like a pre-conceived plan. She is in a low-cut, sleeveless sports dress that falls to just above her knees.

The young man, as soon as he sees her, gives her the once over, then avoids her look.

Ruiz is right, he thinks, *she is pretty and provocative.*

"You can be at ease as far as that's concerned. I only met you last night, and generally the first meeting produces some misunderstanding. We can't judge a person at first sight."

"That's true," she agrees, smiling. Her attitude and focus are different from the day before. "We were pretty disastrous, weren't we. Fortunately, it hasn't stood in the way of getting to know each other better," she affirms with affectation.

They arrive on deck. She picks out two chairs right in the corner of the glass enclosure. There they would be sheltered from the wind, the salt spray and away other people.

The girl picks up where she left off with measured and solemn words. She describes the dance of the previous evening with details supplied by a fertile imagination.

"...the group was wonderful. I didn't stop dancing."

Little does the young man know that she had spent the entire night sitting. There were no boys, and the few that were there were grabbed up and pledged in advance. This was definitely not a voyage for a young girl looking for romantic adventure. Torres represented one of her last hopes.

Accustomed to the widest variety of attentions and endearments, Rosely puts her pride aside and sets out decisively to win over the boy. She is afraid of the brutal monotony of the voyage, and that fact alone is sufficient to break through her initial rejection. But her main reason for this approach is a stubborn desire for revenge that she had been feeding during dance. She can't forget the indifference with which she had been treated. The recovery of her self-esteem would become part of her adventure. She knows, and all too well, the effectiveness of her physical endowments; those natural endowments that, when put to good use, had always had the desired effect. As she sits down, she raises her skirt, letting it rest well above her knees.

The young man is ill at ease. He addresses her politely, but avoids visual contact. With Odete, fortunately, he didn't feel uncomfortable. The memory of her makes him contrast the two. The intellectual gifts of the first vanquish the physical charms of the second. At three o'clock, he excuses himself saying he needs to go to the bathroom, and says goodbye. When he extends his hands, she holds them in hers longer than usual. She smiles, saying:

"See you later, then."

"See you later," he replies, without fully meaning those words.

Rosely perceives that the boy is struggling to escape her feminine wiles. She knows that he is a normal man, but senses that there is something mysterious that keeps him away from sex and decides to probe that anomaly deeply.

Torres, free at last from this unwelcome company, goes to the railing of the ship and searches the marine depths like a seagull. He wants his vision to break through that immensity, and he realizes that it would be easier to do that than to understand women.

He is disillusioned and saddened by the girl's provocation. He knows, despite all his innocence, that the approach of the girl is the outcome of a resolute plan. He cannot discover, however, the purpose of this plan.

The deficiencies of Rosely highlight the virtues of Odete, and he feels great pleasure in remembering that he would be with her shortly.

* * *

Meetings with Ruiz are now at mealtimes. At dinner on this day, Torres, knowing the role that his friend would play in the future, tells him of the adventures that afternoon. The doctor notes that the description of the last contact with Odete reflects much more than the younger man intended to say. *Can it be that they are in love?* he observes with surprise. Suddenly, he remembers an important fact.

"Your affair with Odete is becoming complicated."

"Why?"

"Her mother spoke to me."

"Her mother?!" he exclaims, nearly choking.

"Yes."

"What did she want?"

"She told me about some of her daughter's problems, but I will tell you only after you continue the story about your past. I want to know, after all, the facts that led you into the priesthood."

"It won't do any good for me to be stubborn, will it?"

"You know very well that it won't."

"Very well, but afterward I want to know all the details of your conversation with Odete's mother," he says, more consoled.

"I had been looking forward to a tranquil voyage, preparing my papers for the conference, and now I can't getaway from the two of you. That's a kind of priesthood, wouldn't you agree?"

"That depends... Do you believe in God?"

"Why? Does the priesthood always require a God?"

"Obviously. Otherwise it would be a professional duty. In the priesthood, the practice of good reverts to God. But you haven't answered me."

"I began to believe in God a short while ago. The illogic of everything led me to Him. In the sanitarium, we can feel the soul in the palm of our hand. We try to manipulate it, we do what we want with it, but despite everything, we are not its proprietors. There exists, and I have proven it, a strange force that prevails beyond ours. This is commanded, just as in cybernetics, by remote control."

The waiter clears the soup plate away and puts another in its place. His questions as to the quantity of meats and cooked vegetables interrupt Ruiz for a few moments.

"Come on, tell me about your past."

Torres takes a long pull of wine and looks at the sea through the porthole. Small waves are forming on the ocean's surface. This prolonged image slowly relaxes his spirit.

Chapter VI

"And you, what would you like to specialize in: engineering or medicine?" the student counselor asked him.

In those days there were three professions with a favorable future: law, medicine and engineering. Students who had juridical inclinations were separated at the end of junior high school and attended a classical course. In the last year of the scientific course, diversification became necessary.

Medicine meant biology, and biology meant memorizing names of plants, insects, parts of plants and animals. This memorization would go against his principles of Rousseauism. All that was left was engineering.

"Engineering," he responded, without much conviction.

He thought that his destiny had been defined. He didn't know that his life could have unforeseen detours.

He turned 18 at the beginning of third year scientific classes. Oh! What an age for dreaming. Loftier accomplishments, altruism, presidential dreams and great loves.

In the middle of that year, Torres moved to São Paulo so that he could take a preparatory course for the entrance exams. His father rented a small house in a duplex where he and his older brother, who was in the second year of engineering school, could live.

São Paulo meant freedom from all the restrictions of small town life. He delighted in the daily contact with the dynamism of the big city where there were, among other things, large amounts of people, movement, and girls for future romances.

Torres, driven by all these illusions, began to burn all the energy accumulated in his native town. His face revealed, then, a happy smile.

He arose at six-thirty, ready and willing for the marathon he would follow. He had a quick breakfast of coffee with milk, bread and butter at the corner bar, boarded a streetcar grabbing on to a handrail. The open streetcars exposed passengers to the chill of August. Looking around the streets, he stared at the residences that stared back at him, and watched as they faded into the distance. São Paulo was huge, and he imagined that in the midst of all that vastness, something awaited him.

At seven-thirty he entered the classroom of his preparatory course. Since he had started in mid-year, some of the subject matter had already been partially covered. Because of that, he didn't understand the classes too well. The classroom, built on risers, held 150 students, 150 that he didn't know. He still hadn't made any friendships, but he was little concerned with that. He knew that within a few days, he would be participating in some lively encounters.

After an hour and a half of class, there was a coffee break, and the students would go to a bar. Torres accompanied them and, off in a corner, would see them ordering coconut filled sweet rolls and coffee. After a while, he would order the same from a waiter and enjoy his snack. Afterwards, they returned, he still by himself, his colleagues together in animated talk and laughter.

At noon, he left his notebooks at home and went out to lunch. At the corner there was a boarding house which furnished meals on a daily basis. He sat alone. The others, mostly men, were mainly mechanics from a nearby garage. The meals generally consisted of rice, beans, a rather small steak, salad and bread.

Lunch over, he would go home and lie down a while. The beds were still rumpled for the simple reason that they were never made. The windows were always closed, and a layer of dust could be found here and there.

Usually, at two in the afternoon, he would begin to study the subjects of the course. He had to attend a lot of classes and make up for lost time.

At six, he went out for dinner. The food was the same, the only difference being the inevitable rice balls made from the rice left over from lunch. The lady who ran the boarding house was a good disciple of Lavoisier: "In nature, nothing is created, nothing is lost. Everything is transformed."

Fifteen minutes before seven, he headed toward the public high school where he was still completing the third scientific year. The students in the night classes were generally from less fortunate families; they worked by day and studied at night. As in the college preparatory course, the boy still had not firmed up any relationships with his third year classmates.

The classes began at seven o'clock and finished at 11. Returning home, Torres had to walk seven blocks on foot. Half an hour later he was in bed and quickly fell into a sound sleep happy because he was in São Paulo!

Fifteen days were enough to induce certain observations. *What kind of life is this?! Get up, study, eat and sleep. And what about the dances, parties and romance? Where are they?*

He had tried in the past few days to strike up acquaintances with his classmates in both courses. The dialogs, the ideas and the feelings were quite different from those in the interior. In São Paulo there was a certain amount of egoism in all contacts, and Torres, not having found fertile ground for friendships, wound up withdrawing into his shell. His schedule did not mesh with that of his brother, and in a few weeks he felt himself isolated even though living in the midst of six million inhabitants.

* * *

Two weeks had gone by when, on his way to school, he spotted a girl he knew from Botucatu on the streetcar.

"Sonia!"

The girl looked around, startled, and then smiled.

"What a surprise, you here?!"

Torres let go of the handrail and sat down beside her.

"Where are you living?"

"I'm in a boarding house on Rebouças Avenue, near the Fradique. And you?"

"I live in a house on Cardinal Arco Verde Avenue."

The dialog continues ritualistically. They both feel like recently discovered runaways.

Sonia had been his constant partner at dances at home, but he was surprised when he took in her features now. He thought it strange that she had not changed a bit in those few months when everything became different. The outline and dimensions of her face were exactly the same: medium height, slightly plump, and extremely maternal breasts. He found her quite happy, although he noted a certain sadness in her look.

"Do you miss Botucatu?"

"A lot."

"But what are you doing here?"

"I graduated last year and, as the first in my class, I was chosen to be a teacher in Vila Galvão."

"I remember your graduation very well; you danced the waltz at midnight with your father, didn't you?"

"Yes, I did."

"Are you enjoying São Paulo?"

"To be frank, I don't like it one bit."

"Neither do I!"

"I only have one friend. She's from Bauru and lives with me at the boarding house."

"I thought I was the only one who couldn't make friends... Well, I get off at the next stop. I'll see you around," he says, holding out his hand.

All during class, Torres felt happy. He thought about his meeting with Sonia. It cheered him up.

How beautiful she is!

"You, there... the new boy," called the teacher, pointing at him.

"Me?!"

"Yes, you. Answer me: why is a three-legged table more stable than a four-legged one?"

"Because there are four planes for four points but only one for three points."

"Very good."

The praise left him momentarily satisfied.

Shortly thereafter he remembered that his teacher Peter in Botucatu, had already covered that geometrical problem. He continued, moreover, not being able to get into the rhythm of the preparatory course. The motto of this school, "three years in one", forced him into constant study, impairing his attention at the high school. These preparatory courses were as important as life and death.

At the high school, he had abandoned the subjects unnecessary for the entrance exams, but the teachers of Portuguese and biology insisted he continue to study these subjects, especially because of his large number of errors in Portuguese.

"You," called the teacher of his mother tongue, "what have you read, lately?"

Torres had received two zeros in this subject in three months. The teacher, of great intelligence, so they said, was inordinately proud of the low grades which she graced the students with and which he kept on getting.

* * *

"Maybe this was an act of repression," interrupts Ruiz. "Perhaps she was trying to assert herself and show off to her colleagues. Go on."

* * *

"You received another zero in the weekly review, and I would like to give you a chance to improve your grade."

He vacillated; he had read nothing. Literature didn't fit into his life. Entertainment during the country phase of his life took up all his free time.

"Don't tell me you haven't read anything!"

"Yes, yes I have."

"Then tell me."

Torres looked left and right; his classmates stared back, envious of his cultural activities. He was cut down, he wavered.

His humiliation made him blush intensely. He lowered his head.

"Well, then?" she insisted.

"I read *Iracema* by José de Alencar," he said, remembering a classmate's dissertation from a previous class.

"Just as well," she comments, relieved. "Otherwise... Let's discuss its story line."

The boy looks around him once again, looking for some assistance; nothing, he was truly alone.

"Iracema was an Indian," he stopped. He couldn't figure out a reasonable plot.

"Continue."

"She was also called the 'virgin of the honeyed lips."

Damn! I don't know anything else. What a meddlesome little woman she is. I want to be an engineer, he declares to his wounded self-esteem, *and I'm not interested in any of this literary nonsense.*

He was at the height of his irritation when the bell rang. What divine relief!

"You stay behind, the others may leave."

He obeyed, and his eyes burned into his teacher's arrogant face. He was standing, she was seated. Alone at last!

"You are going to fail for the year," said the teacher, staring like a queen at her subject, "and I don't know what else to do."

"The entrance exams for engineering don't cover Portuguese," he says, innocently, trying to defend himself.

She gets up angrily. Without meaning to, he has offended her four years of college studies. He always ignored the stuffiness of teachers. Their individual subjects were always more important than all the rest.

"What? You are a complete ignoramus!" she shouts, walking towards him.

Torres backs away.

* * *

"I confess that I too am really beginning to be afraid of her," he admits to Ruiz. "The bull was really charging the cape. I think that, as you said, she wanted to lash you, a poor but useful innocent target, with her frustrated old maid complex. Marriage probably seemed a lot of nonsense to her, but Portuguese..."

* * *

She stopped in front of Torres and pointed her finger at him; she was ready to wipe him out with a single blow. He, poor thing, was less than nothing in the order of things.

"I'll have you know... Never mind, you can go. Your grade is still zero," she screamed, consoling herself.

"Torres was shocked, wanting to ask her what happened, but he couldn't. He couldn't understand that impulsive reaction.

"Get out," she screamed, again.

He went out and didn't turn back because of a simple syllogism: If he went back, he would fail the year, and since he didn't want to fail it...

The following day, with his spirits quite low, he transferred to a high school known for its lack of discipline. Obviously, it could only be a private school. This change brought some alterations to his life. To get there, he had to take a streetcar, go into the city, take another streetcar, and then 'hoof it' a couple of blocks.

It was recess the first day of class at the end of October. The following month would be the exams, and he needed very high grades, nearly the maximum allowed. His biology teacher called him in.

"You haven't yet received a grade this month. Do you need much?"

"Plenty high," he answered, wondering.

"How high?"

"Nine," he affirmed, boldly.

"All of that? Very well, you may leave."

Is that all there is to it? he wondered, returning to the courtyard.

But, despite his wonder, he felt relieved. These facts were measuring up to his expectations. He resumed talking to two of his classmates from the preparatory course who were also studying at that school, and felt a glow of well-being spread through his body.

This happiness, however, was short-lived. The first problems surfaced during the next class.

"Teacher," said the monitor at the classroom door, "the office is calling Torres."

Perplexed, the boy gets up and heads toward the office.

"Please sit down," a man said to him with excess politeness. "You have paid our treasurer for the month of October, but August and September are still due."

"Why?" he asked, wonderingly.

"The entire semester must be paid. We only accept students in the final months under those conditions."

"But, I can't, I... don't have the money!"

"If you don't pay the previous two months, you won't be able to take the exams. This must be done by November 15th."

Torres could see that it was no use to argue. He got up and left.

I paid 250 Cruzeiros for October, I have to arrange another 500 Cruzeiros, I have to telephone home...

His whole body sagged. He had made the transfer without telling his parents. His monthly allowance was a thousand Cruzeiros, three hundred for the preparatory course and seven hundred for all other expenses. Practically nothing was left over for diversions, and that had been the main reason that kept him from looking up Sonia.

At the end of that week, which happened also to be the end of the month, he went to Botucatu to ask for an increase in his allowance for the next thirty days. But he couldn't summon up enough courage because he could see that the sacrifices that his parents were making to maintain him and his brother were the straining the income his parents earned as civil servants.

The train on which he was to return to São Paulo had not yet left in station in Botucatu. Torres flung himself down into a window seat and tried to think of a solution when, looking at the seat ahead of him, he saw Sonia taking a tearful farewell from her mother; tears ran from her eyes. The scene moved him deeply.

Shortly thereafter, the train departed, and she, with her face out the window, waved continuously in a long goodbye. Torres, overcome with melancholy, sympathized intimately with Sonia. When the train had rounded a curve soon afterwards, and the station was no longer in sight, she started to sit down and saw him. She nodded to him, trying to hide her reddened eyes with her hands. They were most unhappy.

For more than an hour, the boy thought of some way to approach her. His fertile imagination had found him seated by her side several times. The girl was completely absorbed in reading a novel and gave the impression that she hadn't cried at all.

The attraction he had felt for her previously grew in proportion to the length of the trip. At the end of the first hour, he no longer saw her as simply a dancing partner. Her outburst of at the station, her need for affection, and the settled calm that emanated from her all came together, awakening tenderness within him.

Torres traced out a strategy for approaching her. He would get up, pass by her, go to the end of the car, get a drink of water and, on returning, as he passed by her, would venture a question and bravely sit down at her side.

He got up, passed by her, looked at her out of the corner of his eye, went to the drinking fountain at the door, filled a cup, drank, and firmly began the return journey. As he came near her, he slowed his steps nearly to a halt. Sonia kept on reading and didn't see him. He started to say her name, but lacked the courage and wound up back in his own seat.

Stupid! What an overgrown coward!

He stayed another half hour trying to put together a new tactic. He decided to approach the girl whatever the cost.

Shall I call her from back here? But for what reason? The weather? No, that's dumb! The classes she's giving? No, same reason. Candy! That's it!, he remembered, as though it were a great discovery. *I'll offer her some candy.*

"Sonia, would you... like some candy?"

She looked at him, startled. She smiled and said: "No, thank you."

"Try one. They're quite good."

"All right," she answered, yielding.

The girl had perceived that, if she had kept on refusing, Torres was quite capable of stuffing one into her mouth, such was his determination.

Trembling, the boy unwrapped one and gave her the candy.

"Thank you," she said with a smile.

Torres remained standing in the hope of being invited to sit down. An interminable silence induced him to withdraw. Just as he was about to turn:

"Would you like another?" he offered, desperately. If he continued to act like this, he might very well give her all his candy one at a time to the last one.

"This one is enough, thank you. Would you like to sit down?" she asked, ruefully, seeing him planted like a statue in front of her.

Torres broke out in a wide smile of happiness and hurriedly accommodated himself.

"How are you doing in the preparatory course?"

"All right, I guess. All right."

"You guess?!" she retorted, intently

The girl's self-confidence stirred admiration of her in the boy.

"Well... it's pretty difficult to absorb three years of subject matter in just six months," he said, looking at her with resolve. Her serene expression impressed him.

"And your high school studies?" she continued, closing her book.

"Now they're OK. I changed schools. The other one was too difficult."

"Which school are you in, now?"

"Louis XIV. Everyone passes there. You just have to pay."

"You're smart, eh?"

Torres smiled as though cued in a theater. Recognition of his astuteness puffed up his pride.

"Have you gone out much?" he asked.

"There hasn't been much time. Now and then I go to a movie."

"You haven't gone to any dances?"

"In these three months I have only gone to a birthday party."

"It's a boring life, don't you think? I miss our good old days," she states with melancholy.

The boy was feeling much more at ease. The kilometers were passing by more rapidly.

"It was so hard to get to dance with you!"

"Of course. There were five or six boys for every girl. We, the girls, couldn't be 'wallflowers' even if we wanted to. But when a group of girls from outside arrived, you forgot us, didn't you?"

"Well, you know," he explained, trying to apologize, "new faces, new adventures. And when some boys arrived, didn't you fall for them too?"

"True. Those were good times, weren't they?"

"Oh, yeah..."

A fine rain, accompanied by a strong wind, made the windowpane 'sing' with the raindrops hurled against it. The eucalyptus trees shook, and dry leaves blew across the horizon.

"And have you gone to the movies?" she inquired.

"Only once."

"What film did you see?"

"*The Ghosts.* An English comedy. I liked it very much."

"So did I. These *Company* comedies are wonderful. English humor is very well done by the actors; the director was very good, too."

"Director?!"

At 18, Torres was still unaware of the technical meaning of the word 'director.'

"The work of the actors depends a great deal upon the director. Unaffected cynicism, which is very English, is difficult to portray without the help of a good director."

The conversation was convincing him, little by little, of his inferiority to her. This feeling added to his desire to get to know her better.

"Would you like to go to the movies with us? Miriam and I generally go alone at night, and it would be good to have someone go with us."

"I would like that very much," he answers, euphorically.

The invitation has put new life into the boy. This could be the start, the cornerstone of a future relationship of greater responsibility. He couldn't contain his happiness, but his smile faded when he remembered his growing financial difficulties.

"Don't worry about ticket money. You, like us, must be counting your pennies to scrape by; everyone for himself," said Sonia, guessing the reason behind his hesitancy. "After the movie, we can have a soda and go for a walk."

"Agreed," he answered with relief.

The train arrived and it was time to say goodbye. They separated after a handshake and a slight smile.

The following day, Torres explained to the school treasurer the difficulty he was having to come up with the late payments.

"It's a rule of the school. There's nothing I can do about it. If you don't pay for the semester, you won't be able to continue attending classes."

"But I don't have enough money!"

"As a final choice, I can offer to let you pay two of the months now and the rest in December."

"Isn't there any other way?"

"I'm afraid not."

"Very well, then."

He took five one-hundred cruzeiro notes from his pocket and handed them over. His eyes took in the agility with which the treasurer handled the money. An avaricious smile broke out on the lips of the man who was one of the partners of the establishment.

Torres accepted the receipts, got up, and was leaving when he was called back.

"Don't forget. Next month you will have to pay two monthly installments," he said, rubbing his hands; an intriguing smile adorned his face.

He had only five hundred cruzeiros left and he needed three hundred to pay for the preparatory course. The remaining two hundred would have to due instead of the precarious seven hundred spentduring the preceding months and he had no idea to whom he could turn in this emergency. There was no other solution except to make drastic cuts in his expenses. In the mornings, he had just a cup of coffee; his lunch was usually a *spaghetti with tomato sauce* at a cheap restaurant, and dinner consisted of a large cup of coffee with milk and a roll with butter. He took only one streetcar to the high school, and instead of the second one, he went the rest of the way on foot. He had to walk ten blocks through the worst part of the city.

In two weeks, as a result of this drastic economy, he had managed to spend only 120 cruzeiros. The effects of poor nutrition, the intense rhythm of life and the short nights of sleep were making themselves felt. He was becoming physically and morally debilitated.

Sundays, were the worst days. His brother had his own diversions as a university student, and he continued hardly seeing him. Nostalgia for the dances and flirts in Botucatu overwhelmed him. What used to be the happiest day of the week had turned into the saddest. He generally slept later, then he would go to the restaurant looking for either pasta or soup. He would return home, study until late, dine on the same coffee with milk and a roll with butter, and go to mass at seven o'clock.

One Sunday, in the middle of November, he wanted to telephone Sonia. He didn't, afraid of being invited to go with her to the cinema. The money left for the rest of the month allowed for no extra expenses.

An intense aversion toward everything and everyone came over him. He wanted to change something or do something or at least diminish the monotony of those moments. His loneliness was so great that he felt like talking to himself. His hunger for conversation or a friendly voice drove him into the street. And it was with that feeling that he went to mass.

* * *

"The mass that Sunday," narrates Torres with emotion, "absorbed me completely. I had always been a religious person, but somewhat dissipated. I felt that my loneliness, had been greatly relieved and, once the service was over, I remained kneeling, praying with a faith unknown to me."

His eyes shine and his face glows with a great peace. He remains silent for some time, looking abstractly into space.

"Go on," charges Ruiz. "From what I can see, we are close to the reason that took you to the seminary."

100

"Not yet," corrects the younger man, "a lot of things happened before I decided to become a priest."

* * *

Later on at home, Torres meditates about the comfort he received during mass. That occurrence, however, wasn't completely strange to him. The previous Sunday he had experienced the same feeling, but it had passed almost unnoticed.

Now he kept on thinking about it, dissolving his loneliness completely. He felt, then, that he was no longer an isolated being in the midst of six million people. He had finally found the peace of spirit he had sought since he had arrived in São Paulo.

Nevertheless, he could not define the real reason for all of this. He realized that he was being caught up in something unexplainable and tried to remember the details of the period during which he had been in church. He remembered, then, that there had been something hovering in the air, a kind of companionship had touched the terrible solitude of his soul.

The well-being was still tingling through his body. He felt an urge to get up and go back to church. Just as his urge became strongest, he remembered that, as he was going out the door to leave, the priest was waiting so he could close up. The priest had his hand on the door, and Torres had greeted him meekly and had received a broad, pure smile in return. Happiness had adorned the demeanor of the clergyman, and that contentment had intrigued him greatly.

The priestly life had always seemed to me to be horribly isolated, he had thought at the time. *I had never been able to imagine that a priest could be happy. For me, happiness consisted of dances, flirtations, lots of movies, and strolls. It's a great mystery.*

101

His frown deepened; the doubt was strange to him. He remembered, then, with a certain fondness, the time when sister Theresa had run her fingers through his hair.

I wanna be priest, sister.

Cassock and loneliness. My concept was wrong. There wasn't that much loneliness, there wasn't any loneliness at all.

Then he remembered Sylvia, the destroyer of priestly vocations.

A priest can't get married.

Sylvia's image affectionately brought forth Sonia's. Her lively and intelligent face appeared before him. He got up with her on his mind, took a few steps in the room, and turned on the radio.

But why is that priest happy? he asked himself.

The radio began to play slow, romantic music.

How beautiful Sonia is! Oh! If I could have her here by my side! I could be dancing with her like I did every Sunday. She dances so well!

He went to bed thinking of Sonia. Her face embellished his pillow and, yearning for reality, he nearly kissed it. In a quick flash of emotion, he remembered what he had felt during Mass and fell asleep.

The next morning, at school, he felt a pleasant well-being for a few moments. Every since he had switched high schools, he had dedicated himself completely to this course. His grade in the last test had improved somewhat, but he was still far from being an average student.

Lunch that day was unendurable. The *spaghetti in tomato sauce* was repugnant to him. He longed for good steak with French fries which he had seen the waiter take to the table in front of him. The little tables covered with square-cut tablecloths and stained with sauce, and the stale smelling surroundings made the place repellent. Lunch goes down his gullet; he rises and leaves.

At home, he turned on the radio and laid down for a while. The repugnance he had felt gave him an urge to abandon everything and go back home. He could no longer stand the hunger, the sleepiness and the lack of diversion. At the height of his revulsion, he remembered once again the episode at church the day before. The sensation of companionship that he had encountered there took hold of him. He could feel that something indefinable was drawing near him, but sleep dominated him, and he slept for an hour. The alarm clock was his implacable enemy.

In the afternoon, he decided to have a snack on the way he took on foot to go to school. Along the way there was a restaurant that served meat pies and sausages.

* * *

"It was there that Rosa appeared," says Torres.

"Who is she?" Ruiz asks.

"Rosa was a young girl of the street who had a profound influence on my vocation."

"How so? A woman of the street?!" he exclaims, disturbed.

The gong for the second sitting at dinner interrupted them. Coffee had already been served some time ago.

The waiter motions to them, and they get up to leave and a few recalcitrant companions like themselves accompany them to the exit.

Chapter VII

"Let's go," presses Odete, "or else we'll miss the baptizing."

"This hat won't stay on my head," complains Torres, bending over to pick up a straw hat which had fallen off for the second time.

And with that, they run down the corridor hand in hand. The master of ceremonies has given repeated warnings over the loudspeaker for the participants in the 'ceremony' not to be late.

When they arrive, the revelers are already celebrating around the pool. In general, they are wearing costumes made out of crepe paper, worn over their swimsuits. It is a hot, clear day. The cold wind which had accompanied them on the greater part of the voyage had stopped completely.

About 20 couples, encircled by a rope, begin to dance. The spectators encourage them, and the atmosphere is turning festive.

Torres and Odete watch from a corner. He still can't decide whether to participate in the party. He has felt this hesitation ever since he first heard of this diversion. The girl had to make up several arguments to persuade him to take part in the entertainment. When she finally got him to agree, she ran up against another obstacle: he didn't want to wear

104

the red sarong she had made for him. Odete had made another just like it for herself, only in white paper. Serpentines and confetti are being thrown. The hubbub of the crowd drowns out her voice and she must shout in Torres' ear, trying to encourage him. When they at last cross over to the ropes, the dancing has stopped and the partygoers are jumping over Neptune's trident. This carnival-like costume is by far the best and belongs to the leader of the festivities. The trident shines in the sun light and waves in rhythm like an orchestra leader's baton. The band is playing marches, and the cries in various languages nearly drowns it out. At a glance, it is easy to see that most of the enthusiasm comes from the Brazilians who happen to make up the largest group.

After a while when the sweaty bodies are covered with serpentines and confetti, the leader orders the music to stop and gives instructions in several languages.

Those passengers who have never been baptized – he advises in very poor Portuguese – will be obliged pass by him and jump into the pool. Only at the conclusion of this ceremony will the others be able to join them.

"Whoever has already been baptized cannot jump in yet," he affirms, waving his enormous fork.

The view outside the ship doesn't change: sea and sky, and nothing else. The line of the equator passes under the ship; it divides south from north, and it is Torres' first time in the north.

"Everyone line up here," continues Neptune. "Anyone who resists will be baptized by force."

Some ten people hurriedly line up in front of him and the ceremony begins. The guide, as part of the ritual, places the crown on the 'pagan,' and orders that he hold the trident for a few moments, and then pushes him into the pool.

The spectators laugh uproariously as they see the individual struggling and climbing up the ladder soon after with paper clinging to his body. And so it goes, one by one, until the last. Torres is not in the group.

"Are there any more volunteers?" asks the leader through a megaphone.

No one appears.

"Now, all those who know of the existence of 'pagans' in our company have the obligation to denounce them under penalty of the rain that I shall send for the rest of the trip around Europe.

"Here's one," shouts a woman, pointing to her husband.

Her companion, a bald man of about 40 years, looks at her in shock as she laughs wholeheartedly. He looks as though he is ready to leave in a hurry, but he is stopped by the people behind him.

"I want three volunteers," asks Neptune.

More than five step forward, happily. Expectation is palpable. The guide chooses the three strongest, and all four proceed to where the man is being held. They grab him with some difficulty by the arms and legs and carry him to the edge of the pool. Neptune places the crown on the belly of the 'unfortunate one,' gives him a shove, and they throw him into the water.

After that, the accusations become more frequent, the exits are blocked, and no-one escapes the wrath of the 'priest.'

At one point, Odete raises her hand and accuses Torres. Neptune has his back turned and doesn't see her.

"No, Odete!" pleads the young man, trying to lower her hand. "Don't do that!"

"He hasn't been baptized, yet," she says, laughing out loud and paying no attention to his pleas.

106

Her voice rises above the rest, and the people surround him and began to shout, pointing at him.

"Odete, don't do this," he complains, frightened.

The shouting gets the attention of Neptune, and he heads over that way. He asks for another four volunteers, because the first ones are worn out from all the carrying, and they grab him. Torres kicks out, trying to free himself. Then they ask for more help and five persons carry him, wriggling, to the edge of the pool. The terrified look of the young man provokes jovial comments around him. Odete laughs so hard she is crying.

The helpers, after placing the crown over his midsection, heave him into the water. The splash pushes water to the edges. Torres swims to the ladder and climbs up with only his swimsuit because his costume, like so many others, has fallen apart.

"Why did you do that?" he reprimands her.

"Did you want me get rained on all over Europe?" she apologizes, smiling.

The young man calms down and, suggesting they get out of there, goes to the railing in front of the deck bar.

"I think you should have a drink," she advises.

"I'll go get one. Would you like one, too?"

The girl agrees. He goes to the bar and returns a few minutes later with two martinis.

"Here you are," he says, holding out the glass.

"Are you angry?" asks Odete, looking over her companion's face.

"No, I'm cold."

"Why don't you take a hot shower?"

"Later. I want to stay here a little longer."

Torres rests his arm on the armrest and remains silent for a few moments. The ocean surface is calm. There is no wind.

"Can you imagine the caravels on a day like this?" he observes after a while. "They would be completely motionless."

"Sailing has gained many mechanical advantages over the past, but they are not poetic."

"What do you mean by that?"

"It used to be that crossing the ocean was an adventure with the unknown. No-one knew what lay ahead: wind for the sails or murderous storms. The sailors had to scrutinize nature minute by minute and, on a day like this, when the wind stopped, they could meditate in profound silence.

"Poetry or prose?"

"Neither. What saddens me is to see safety and speed coupled to the noise and this constant droning of the motors.

"This is the only way we can have our creature comforts!" he protests.

"But in exchange for our peace of mind."

"I'm going to take a hot shower. Are you going to stay here?"

"No, I'm going below and change out of this costume."

Torres accompanies her to her cabin. On the way, they run into other tourists who talk happily about the adventures of the 'baptism.'

* * *

"Just why did Odete's mother want to see you?" asks Torres as soon as the doctor sits down to lunch. His curiosity is quite real.

"Yesterday, when you were reading in one of the lounge chairs on deck..."

* * *

"Are you related to that young man who shares your cabin?" asked the lady, approaching him purposefully.

"No, I met Torres a few days ago," answered Ruiz, surprised. "Would you like to sit down?," he invited, getting up and at the same time pulling over a chair.

"Thank you," she acknowledged with exaggerated politeness. "I'm the mother of the girl whom he has been meeting during the voyage. You have seen her, haven't you?"

"Torres introduced us."

"If you will allow me, I'll go straight to the point that made me look you up."

"By all means, madam."

"Maria Ramos Penteado is my name."

"Alvaro Ruiz, at your service."

Mrs. Penteado, a lady of impressive appearance, was still beautiful at the age of 45. Her face with its discreet make-up, her well-coifed hair, and her well cut dress made her attractive. Her somewhat hardened appearance guarded her against any eventual danger. Her fetching smiles were faked.

Ruiz' long years of professional practice equipped him for dealing with the most diverse personalities. Nevertheless, the politeness and measured exaggeration of certain persons irritated him. He knew that deceit and hypocrisy were hiding behind that smiling mask.

"Dr. Ruiz, as a mother I am obliged to look out for my daughter.'

"I understand."

"I do not believe in sudden fancies. Romance in today's world represents the incorporation of certain social factors. The economic situation and the family require close attention as a preliminary step. Am I making myself clear?"

"Perfectly."

"My daughter has shown an increasing interest in this young man... Fernando, is that his name?"

"Yes, it is."

"My questions to Odete have frequently been answered evasively. From what little she has told me, I have perceived the existence of a mysterious aura hovering about him. You, as his cabin mate, could, as a special favor, fill me in with more facts. But, perhaps you see my curiosity as an impertinent intrusion?"

"Absolutely not, my dear lady. I recognize that you have a certain right to this," added the doctor, solicitously.

Ruiz took off his glasses and faced his interlocutor, trying to resist the underlying issue. She looked away and her frown deepened. She was a little afraid.

"Your comprehension makes this much easier, and I am grateful. Would you be able, then, to clear up some of my doubts?"

"Madam, I think I can be of little help to you."

"But, as his companion for several days, he must have told you who he is, where he lives."

"I know almost nothing about Torres. I think I have talked to him much more than I have listened."

Odete's mother is disappointed. The inquiery, as she had foreseen, was encountering obstacles. She decided to change the tone of her questions and check out Odete's sparse comments.

"He is a teacher of philosophy, isn't he?"

"A teacher? Oh, yes, he is a teacher of philosophy," he confirmed, vacillating.

"I think you are having some difficulty in helping me. I appreciate the time you have given me. Goodbye," she said coldly taking her leave. As she was about to get up...

"I'm sorry my explanations haven't helped you. Perhaps it's because I really don't know many details about Torres' life," he said, trying to appease her.

She calmed down and felt that she could continue the conversation. Some further information or commentary would most certainly be forthcoming to fulfill her purpose.

"Does he have any vices?"

"I can answer that by what I know of his character; his integrity is unimpeachable."

"Dr. Ruiz," she said, with a certain gravity, "Odete told me that you are a psychoanalyst, so I think you will understand the main reason that made me talk to you. So that you might better understand, I must tell you about some personal reminiscences.

Continuing, she explains at length and in detail the consequences of her unhappy marriage.

"...and my daughter suffered greatly when I confessed to her the reason for my husband's 'trip'."

"It is a most difficult situation."

She smiled in appreciation.

"My pride has stopped me from opening up to others, so if I do so now to you, it is because of your profession."

Ruiz has discerned that the long narrative is over. The curiosity to scrutinize the details minutely had been almost unbearable, but he had known that any interference on his part might have broken the flow of the story.

"Dear lady, allow me to present you with how I understand the matter. The simplest things are often not easy to understand, and the mind uses logical reasoning on these occasions. The disillusion with and disbelief in marriage, brought on by a separation, are felt by the entire family. The situation in which you and your daughter found yourselves, and continue to find yourselves, is very typical. Your concept of matrimony has led you to impose a profound examination upon any potential suitors. Without these little details you would not be able, as you have stated, to be certain of a happy future. But these examinations have proven to be too demanding, the suitors have been exposed as unworthy, and the result was imminent: the flirtations of your daughter have all ended in nothing."

"But then how could we ever be certain of a successful marriage?" she asked, as if only she knew the answer.

"Madam, nothing would lead you to certainty. There are always risks, and they must be dealt with."

"Dr. Ruiz, I had hoped to obtain some information regarding Fernando from you. Now, I think I can put my mind at ease. I am quite sure that you would not deny me any clarification in the future, even if it were to impair the concept my daughter has of this young man."

The doctor felt uncomfortable with the situation. He didn't agree with the reasoning used by Odete's mother, but he couldn't help but warn her against some future disillusion by the daughter.

"Mrs. Penteado," he said, seriously, "another danger that you are unaware of threatens your daughter, and you both should be alerted about it."

"What danger is that?" she asked with affliction.

"That of lack of continuity."

"Why?! ...And ...is he married?" she stammered. "Does he have some physical problem?!" she asked at the same time, revealing her apprehension.

"Torres is single and physically perfect," he explained, serenely. "You must understand young people; they are somewhat tempestuous."

"I am completely confused."

"How can I explain it to you?" he interjects, seeking clarification. "Let us say that Torres is a philosopher and that he has no deep conviction regarding marriage. Perhaps he does not see marriage and fatherhood as the natural consequences of the human being."

"I confess that I am somewhat confused. Do you mean that the young man fears the responsibilities of marriage?"

"In other words, yes. I think you have grasped the idea."

* * *

"I had to lead her to the conclusion that she and her daughter should not nourish great expectations," explains Ruiz to Torres. "When she left, she was worried."

"Odete had already told me about her mother, but your description has shown that her problem is much more complex that I had imagined."

"We are in a dilemma. To carry on with this farce may result in serious harm to this young woman. To break it off might leave you with traces of an unfinished struggle."

"Perhaps my seeing Odete is not a farce," he comments, hesitatingly.

"What do you mean by that?"

"I can't define the type friendship that links me to her. What for me was little more than a playful come-on has taken on a different meaning."

"Torres, I have to tell you that we must act with extreme caution. Any carelessness on your part might be harmful to her."

The waiter, accustomed to the long dialogs at that table, hovers about threateningly. His severe looks and the clearing of his throat have not had their usual results. He has to prepare the table for the next sitting, and these recalcitrant passengers have left him irritable.

"Gentlemen, please, I must set the table for the second dinner sitting."

They get up unwillingly and realize that they are the last ones to leave. Ruiz even takes a sip of wine; his serenity exasperates the waiter.

Their dialog continues in the day room lounge. Some passengers play checkers, chess and cards while others talk energetically. This picture is well-known to them both, and for that reason they waste no time in a closer examination of their surroundings.

"Dr. Ruiz, I have thought a great deal about this. I want to ask you an important question about my feelings for Odete. Do you think that the pleasure I take in her company and the affection that I feel for her may represent something more serious?"

"What is happening to you is absolutely normal. As yet there is no great love nor could there be. The six years that you have spent closed up in the seminary have kept you from any feminine contact. And the moment that you do experience it, you are unprepared to analyze it."

"This girl has suffered so much that I believe my conscience would not live in peace were I to cause her more harm," he states with concern.

"You, and nearly all priests, are ordained unprepared psychologically to confront, not the problems of others, but

114

the occurrence of those dramas within yourselves. You cannot differentiate pity from affection," he comments with authority. "You still have your life ahead of you, and this is a step of supreme importance not to be taken lightly."

Silence looms. Over them they didn't even notice the idiomatic babble of several languages that were all jumbled together in the room. Ruiz resumes speaking after a while.

"The best solution at the moment is to let some time go by. Don't make any definitive resolution for the time being," he insists.

They take their leave of each other. Ruiz goes to the game room. His bridge partners have already set up another rubber. Rosely's parents feel humiliated by the two previous defeats, and the doctor, hoping to console them, intends to let them win this match. He thought that he had arrived late and, to his surprise, his friends were not there. Rosely is waiting for him, however.

"Since you were taking so long, my parents and Mr. Costa went to buy some things at the shops," she explains. Her freckled face breaks out in a smile.

"Thank you. I shall go look for them."

"Wait," she says, interrupting, "won't you sit down for a moment. I'd like to ask you some questions."

"Certainly. I'm at your service."

"Have you known that young man very long?"

"You're the second person to ask me that, today!"

"Who was the other?"

"I'm not sure how to explain; she's the mother of the young lady that he met a few days ago."

"The girl he's been seeing?"

"Do you know her?"

"I have seen them together a few times. They seem to be very much taken with each other. Ever since I met him, I have been intrigued by something: there is something mysterious about him."

"Do you have some interest in that regard?"

"Just curiosity," she answers, offhandedly. "Could you clear up a few details?"

"Your interest in him surprises me. I can't imagine why you should be so concerned."

"Well, as I said, it's just curiosity. Something inexplicable is holding back his sexual impulse. When we talk, I can tell you quite frankly, I feel like I'm in the presence of a priest."

"A priest?!"

"Yes, a priest! An ordinary young man of his age simply does not act that way. When he is beside me, I can see that he is fighting against his instincts. He hasn't really looked me straight in the eyes."

"Torres is a philosopher," explains the doctor with some relief, "and he prides himself on self control of all his bodily reactions."

Rosely is astute, and she could see the dismay of the doctor as he revealed the hypothesis that he had constructed. The alacrity with which he justified Torres' actions told her she was on the right track. Her desire for revenge became even stronger. She was not used to snubs, nor was she accustomed to being passed over in favor of someone like Odete. She knows that her rival is not her physical equal, and this humiliated her.

"Dr. Ruiz, I think you're having some difficulty explaining this mystery."

"You're just being stubborn," he replies a little acrimoniously, "the boy already has enough problems to face;

116

leave him alone. Now, if you'll excuse me, I shall go look for your parents. Goodbye."

Who does he think I am?! thinks Rosely, seething with hatred. *I have never been treated this way. Oh! I'll get even with him. I'll find out the reason for his behavior, whatever the cost.*

* * *

Torres avoids going to the ship's chapel. He knows that his sudden human resolution to continue feeding his affection for Odete does not break any rules of the Church. Despite this conviction, he doesn't have the strength to meet with God.

His contacts with the girl are anxiously awaited. He remembers an episode prior to going into the seminary when he enjoyed all the youthful emotions. Remembering his flirtations of the time, he recognizes that there is no comparison possible between this feeling and the previous ones.

Despite having identified himself as a teacher of philosophy, he avoids more intelligent conversation with her on the subject. He might reveal certain facts or opinions between the lines of some commentary that would betray his real identity.

As to Odete, as soon as she met Torres, she had started to practice her gifts of poetry. But, when feeling her first emotions for the young man, she remembered the criticism of an ex-boyfriend. This ancient suitor had defined her as a disagreeable companion, and the main reason for that was her constant recitation of poems.

Their souls, charged with affection, converse like two beings in love.

* * *

Torres, after his conversation with Ruiz, heads toward the Promenade Deck where he is to meet with Odete to hear the day's musical performance entertainment. He is ten minutes late and he goes up the stairs almost running.

Odete is already waiting for him over in a corner. In her hands she holds a glass with an excessively green liquid.

"Hello, there!" she greets him, "you're late again!"

"Dr. Ruiz tied me down with a long story, and I couldn't leave until the end," he apologizes.

"Well, it's not serious," she amends.

Torres pulls up a chair and sits down. The trio – piano, drums and bass – plays romantic music. The small tables are all taken, and for that reason, several couples sit on the deck. Some of the young people are holding hands, and the heads of the girls rest on the shoulders of the boys. The silence is complete. The short conversation between Odete and Torres brings baleful looks. The crash of the waves made by the ship is heard as a sonorous background. An easy enchantment falls over the softly lit surroudings.

"Would you like a mint cooler?" Odete whispers into her companion's ear.

"Not now, maybe later," he answers in the same tone.

The couple ahead of them looks back reproachfully. They keep quiet and look at each other smilingly. She places a finger to her lips.

"Shh!"

They remain in complete silence for a long time, and, during that time, they both feel united by a strong bond. They feel, then, the desire to meditate together for the first time and the promises made a few days ago are forgotten.

Like good friends, she had said.

Like good friends, he had completed.

Their relationship has now taken on a much more intimate characteristic than friendship.

The musicians stop for a moment, and loud applause can be heard. They resume with 'Stella by Starlight.' A few couples begin to dance, but there is little space since the room is full.

Odete, looking to one side, sees the railing of the ship taken up by curious young people. She takes Torres' hand and they head over there; with some effort, they manage to find an opening.

The ocean surface reflects the moon, making a luminous and wavy path right up to the ship. The plankton, stirred up by the bow of the ship, leave a long, glowing wake that fades far aft, behind the stern.

They both remain silent, but their hands are intertwined. The bond which had grown a short while ago is a feeling of mutual completion that inexorably overwhelms them.

"All passengers," announces the loudspeaker, startling them, "the dance will begin one hour from now, and the next movie session will start in ten minutes."

The trio stops and the couples begin to stir. The murmur of that moment collides with the silence of a short while ago.

"I'm going to get ready for the dance," says Odete, almost shouting into the young man's ear. "What a shame the music had to end," she declares on their way to the cabin.

Torres agrees with a nod of his head; his silence reflects the seriousness of the moments of meditation.

She refrains from speaking and the walk is made in silence; their hands, however, remain entwined.

* * *

The lilting music is contagious. The ballroom is wonderfully decorated with lanterns, serpentines and confetti. The clothes are simple, showing neither extravagance nor exaggerated elegance. The most common dress is slacks with blouse or shirt. Torres and Odete are dressed this way.

The Festival Ballroom is full of people, some dancing very close, others more apart. There is no set pattern.

Torres and Odete dance slightly away from this tumult. The entwined hands and thouching cheeks show that he feels the same emotions as those of eight years ago.

After awhile, the conductor stops the band, the lights go up, and he asks the passengers to clear the dance floor. He then announces that a pair of Spanish dancers will perform.

The girl enters clicking her castanets and dancing around the boy who tap dances and claps in cadence with the music. A few minutes later he begins to sing in an unintelligible dialect; his voice is extremely high. The audience accompanies them with clapping and *olé's*, and, as the rhythm increases, so does the excitement of the spectators.

The next number is an allegory of the bullfights. The girl, dressed with an imitation bull's head, charges the 'valiant' toreador. The boy shows the cape, and, after the girl makes a pass, he turns on his heels, wrapping himself in the red cloth. When the 'bull' starts to charge again, the dancer unrolls himself, but, at the exact moment in which he would be struck, he jumps aside and, with arms extended, holds up the cape to threatening horns.

The number finished, the speaker introduces a musical ensemble of four *carioca* mulattos. They use a *cuica,* a large bass drum, and two tambourines to strike up a throbbing Brazilian samba. The audience is enchanted with the performers who, tambourines in hand, dance around jiggling their hips with mastery.

Some of the passengers begin to dance about between the tables with their arms high and wide. When the mulatto with the bass drum begins to sing traditional carnival songs, there's not a single Brazilian who isn't caught up in the excitement. The rhythm, irresistible to them, takes them into the center of the ballroom and, for the second time on this voyage, they loudly sing together the well-known songs of past carnivals.

The other spectators watch all of this confusion somewhat taken aback. Little by little, however, they start accompanying the music with a 'la, la, la', their inhibition melts away, and soon they are dancing about and shouting with the others.

Torres and Odete participate in all this commotion. His initial resistance is undermined to the point that he joins in with the general excitement. His pre-priesthood status has been forgotten, and nothing else exists for him except the music and Odete. Their hands are firmly entwined, making them feel that a mysterious fluid is rushing through them.

Those young girls who have not yet been fortunate enough to find a partner, look sadly around the ballroom. Because there are so few boys on board, they are destined to make the entire Atlantic crossing without being able to treasure the memory of a fling on the open sea.

Rosely, despite her beauty and exuberance, finds herself among the wallflowers. Her vengeful eyes follow the gyrations of Torres and Odete. She still cannot understand the reason for his preference, especially since her rival is on the ugly side and too skinny.

An hour later, exhausted, they leave the ballroom and head toward the deck. The glass-enclosed part is full of couples. They have no other alternative but to rest their elbows on the open railing facing the sea.

The soft lights, the reflection of the moon and the stars, and the cool breeze that that brushes their faces move some couples to romanticism demonstrated by kisses and embraces.

Torres and Odete gaze at each other silently. In an appropriate moment, as though magnetized, he takes the girl's face in his hands and kisses her. She returns the kiss tenderly and a second kiss is exchanged, uniting them amorously. They are transformed, into beings divested of reason. But, moments later, Torres feels like he has been shaken by strong hands, his eyes take on a terror-stricken look. He has gone beyond the limits stipulated by his conscience at the beginning of the test. He fears now, and rightly so, that he won't be able to control the emotions that are burgeoning within him. Plans for the priesthood and eight years spent in seclusion conflict with the present situation, causing Torres to fear the imminent defeat of his vocation. And Odete is far too deeply attracted to him, unable to accept such an eventual revelation passively.

He, perturbed and not knowing what to do, suggests that he walk her to her cabin. As they go down the stairs, their hands are no longer united.

* * *

Torres is still meditating when, through the porthole, he sees the first signs of daylight. The dawn awakens him from the dream state created by the incident. He draws the curtain, turns over, and sleeps.

Odete, however, remains awake, recriminating herself for not having shared her doubts with the boy. The mystery that envelops him takes on staggering proportions. She falls asleep only when the sun is up, spreading itself throughout the sky.

In between dreams, she hears the well spaced calls of the loudspeaker, although a loud knock on the door is what finally awakens her. Her mother opens it quickly; a feminine voice is heard almost inaudibly. Odete, giving little importance to her mother's return, turns over and goes back to sleep.

* * *

A sea voyage, where there is little to occupy the spirit, produces a peculiar impression. Personal contact is much more frequent than on land. The repeated encounters seem to precipitate events, compressing them into a single adventure without continuity.

* * *

That day, Odete arrives earlier at pool side than her friend. They were to have met at 2:00 and she, 15 minutes early, was already waiting for him. Few people, normal for that hour, passed by.

There is nothing that can interrupt her obfuscated meditation. Her mother's voice, vigilante of the slightest threats against her daughter, preferably masculine ones, still rings in her ears:

"That boy you are seeing is a priest."

"A priest? Impossible! Like always, you always find something wrong with my friends," accuses Odete, heatedly. Her surprise is enormous.

"This morning a young girl came by, on the pretext of doing me a great favor, and revealed this astonishing truth.

I was almost certain that there was something odd about that boy."

"It's a lie! Who is this girl? I want to talk to her."

"She didn't say who she was, but, by her description, I have no doubts. That boy is really a priest."

"It's a lie, a lie, it can't be," she protests, vehemently. Her eyes fill with tears.

"It's true, my dear. The talk I had with Dr. Ruiz helped me to believe in this girl."

"But, mother, don't you see that this might be a conspiracy."

"I know that it is not," she answers, trying to convince her with a strong tone of voice. "From now on I won't allow you to see this scoundrel. Since when have you ever seen such a thing, a priest going out with a woman! It's the end of the world; he should be ashamed of himself, and..."

"That's enough, mother. Don't start making unjust demands on me. This is one of the times I agree with father: it is very difficult to live with you."

A long silence makes itself felt. Shortly, she opens a drawer, takes out a handkerchief, and leaves, slamming the door behind her.

* * *

It's not possible, she thinks now at the pool. *Torres a priest?*

But she well knows that it may very well be a great and terrible truth. The pieces of the puzzle fall easily into place. Everything takes its proper place and leads to a single conclusion.

And how can I say this to him? She thinks, walking around the pool. *I can't just undo everything all at once.*

124

The minutes go by, and Torres arrives.

"Did you have a good night?" she asks without looking at him.

"I only fell asleep in the morning."

"And what time did you get up?"

She can't make up an intelligent conversation. Her worries about Rosely's accusation hold her back.

"Dr. Ruiz woke me at lunch time. But why all this curiosity?"

"Just curiosity," she answers, not facing him yet.

"You're being a little mysterious. Did something happen?"

Odete seems to be searching for an idea or a secret word. She breathes deeply and looks at him fixedly.

"I don't know how to say this," she speaks in an extremely serious tone. "A young girl looked up my mother and told her you're a priest."

"What? A priest? Me?"

"Yes."

A dreadful silence occurs. Torres doesn't know what to say; this revelation is unexpected, and he isn't prepared to make explanations regarding his vocational status. He had intended to clarify these facts at the end of the voyage, not now. He feels like lying to get out of the dilemma, but he perceives that he cannot think only of himself.

"I am not a priest," he states, energetically.

"I'm so glad!" she says, relieved. "I almost believed it. You're not..."

"But I may be one very shortly," he confesses, interrupting the girl who, overwhelmed with joy, is babbling on.

"Are you a seminarian, then?" she asks with a faint smile.

"Yes, I am to be ordained within a few months."

"And I... that is, we..." she stammers without being able to finish the sentence.

"Do you remember when I told you about my case of frustrated love?"

"Yes, I do."

"I made it all up at that time. That was the reason why I didn't want to continue with our friendship."

"But I thought it was a real love and I set out to destroy it. I even thought that I was setting you free."

"That day, when we agreed to behave as good friends, I couldn't imagine that things would get to this point. Later, with a heavy conscience, I wanted to tell you about my situation, but Dr. Ruiz stopped me."

"But what does Dr. Ruiz have to do with this?"

"He's the one who thought up this absurd situation... or rather, this whole drama. He explained to me the benefits of an amorous test before I took my final vows. In the beginning, I accepted his ideas just to get rid of his insistence; then I approved his idea wholeheartedly. When I wanted to end everything, he disagreed, alleging that vestiges would remain from an unfinished effort, and it was better to let the test go on.

"I can understand my part in all this, although what I can't understand is how you could get to the point of embracing and kissing me without being so inclined. Was that also part of the plan?"

The boy tries to recompose himself mentally. He leaves the girl at the pool, walks over to the railing, and gazes at the depths of the ocean. The meditation furnishes him with the answer that he sought: he turns and motions Odete to join him.

126

"Do you see where the sky meets the sea?" he asks, pointing at the horizon.

"Yes, but why?"

"Don't take your eyes off it until I am finished with what I have to say to you."

She agrees, and Torres begins to tell her the reasons that led him into the priesthood, and the motives that induced him to take that test. The description is quite detailed, and after an hour, he concludes.

"I want to confess, with complete assurance, that there was no betrayal in my manifestations of affection," he speaks with great effort, searching for the right words.

Odete, despite her anxiety, avoids interrupting him. She knows that the definition of the young man's feelings for her are quite near.

"When our togetherness became more intimate, I discovered that I wasn't sure of the outcome. I had reached a crossroads of the two paths open to me, and I didn't know which one to follow. I acted, then, like a boyfriend without a true conviction in marriage. Do you understand?"

"More or less. You mean that people in love can kiss without being certain that it will end in marriage."

"In other words."

"But our case is different. There is no human factor at stake, but a divine one!"

"In the beginning I also thought that way, but Dr. Ruiz explained to me that the struggle was not between you and God but between you and the priesthood."

They remain silent. Odete thinks about finding a solution. Torres sits down, relieved at having revealed himself while apprehensive at the same time as to the future of his relationships.

"I admit that I was hurt, but now, after your explanation, I can see that there was no hypocrisy on your part."

"Does that mean that we can continue our friendship?"

"At this point, I think that our relationship is no longer that of a simple friendship, don't you agree?"

"I do."

"We can't go on with our love, knowing that you are in a constant struggle with your conscience as a seminarian. Either you choose me or the Church."

"Odete, don't be hasty. I was only going to weigh the facts when we got to Naples."

"Don't you understand? It's impossible for me. I... I can't stay with you without that certainty; we wouldn't be acting like normal people, and, accordingly, we wouldn't prove anything."

Torres looks down and sees the waves thrown up by the bow as it plows into the sea. The first ones, with the impact, die as though they had never existed. Everything, then, has its consequence, everything has a reason for its existence in the order of things.

"I must tell you that your answer won't imply any matrimonial pledge."

He hears and remains silent. Shortly, he looks at her fixedly and says,

"I'll meet you here tomorrow at this same time. By then I will decide which path I will follow."

* * *

Torres takes the girl to her cabin and begins to walk aimlessly about the ship. He goes up and down stairways, he goes to the bar and has an aperitif. He avoids analyzing hypotheses, but he cannot shut out the dilemma for long.

He gets up, bewildered, and heads toward the cinema. The film is an Italian comedy and he, along with the other spectators, enjoys some good laughs. The dialog of the artists is often not well understood, but the gestures and typical Latin eloquence makes up for this defect with relative ease.

He leaves the amphitheater two hours later with the problem half forgotten. He tries to maintain himself as free as possible from distractions, for he knows that he must make a decision, even though the paths open to him are very equal.

The gong of the loudspeaker sounds and the announcer declares the beginning of first sitting for 'pranzo.' The young man picks up his pace and quickly crosses through the ship's labyrinth of corridors.

* * *

"...and it's because of your broad experience that I have told you of the dilemma in which I find myself," says Torres to Ruiz, concluding his commentary on his two alternatives.

"Truly, you are still quite young to have to choose one of the paths with wisdom. You did well in consulting me. Besides, I feel responsible for your future. When I proposed the test to you, I confirmed that you were, perhaps unconsciously, undecided concerning your vocation. Remember that time about your clerical collar?"

"Yes, I do."

"Now that we are at this crossroads, you must tell me the reasons that led you to the seminary. Make an effort and give me the main details."

The doctor takes a sip of wine and cuts a piece of veal.

"After your story, we will have a long conversation, most of the night."

The young man eats distractedly. His attention is fixed on Ruiz' face.

"Unfortunately," he proceeds, "it won't be possible to keep up this drama until the end of the voyage."

They grow silent. The murmur of the dining room makes itself heard, as if their hearing had been interrupted for long moments.

Chapter VIII

That night, on the way home from school, he went into a restaurant and sat down at a small table in the corner.

The waiter, in a dirty apron and with long, grimy fingernails, went over to him and took out a pad of paper from his pocket.

"What'll ya' have t'eat?"

"Two sausage sandwiches, two cheese pastries, and a cup of coffee with milk," he said with chronic hunger.

The waiter wrote down the order and contemptuously walked away.

Torres, raising his eyes, perceived that he was being watched. Some scantily dressed and overly made-up young girls at neighboring tables were watching him. Their puffy eyes reflected the faligue of orgiastic nights.

Wondering why he had aroused this attention, he looked at his clothes searching for some abnormality; the wrinkled shirt and shabby slacks, however, couldn't be the reason for such careful examination.

The prostitutes continued to stare at him. He counted the number of tables: there were three and there were two girls at each one.

Their curiosity satisfied, the girls, as if by command, returned their attention to their plates. Their dinner was a

131

kind of blue-plate special and consisted of rice, beans, and a stew of meat and potatoes. The silence was broken only by trivial comments, nothing else. Now and then, one of them would catch him watching them. An inviting smile flashed at him, and he averted his eyes very quickly.

The waiter brought his food. The sausages were squeezed into the bread as though they were trying to escape, covered by a thick tomato sauce. The cold, greasy pastries were off to one side. Clots floated grotesquely in his coffee with milk.

The prostitutes looked his dinner; experience had also put them through hard times and, therefore, they looked away without condescension. He was no longer a source of curiosity or business. Torres, humiliated, lowered his eyes and began to eat the wretched food. His hunger, stronger than revulsion, forced him to eat it all.

He had grown accustomed to seeing those marketplace glances on his daily trek to the high school. *Look, look, come see and buy the best of the…,* he imagined a pitch man shouting at the top of his lungs.

Now they were no longer simply merchandise on display. The act of eating had brought to the surface, perhaps unconsciously, their human dignity. They raised their eyes, to be sure, at the slightest sound, but, when they had their heads down, they behaved like ordinary, decent human beings. Dejection, however, lined their faces.

One of the young girls kept him under constant surveillance; their eyes met several times. Torres didn't know why she watched him in a different way than the others.

Having finished his snack, he paid the waiter and was leaving when, passing by her, she grabbed his arm.

"Wouldn't you like to sit down, honey?" she asked, sweetly.

132

She was alone and waiting for him, the others having left moments before.

"I can't. I'm late," he answered, calming himself.

"Just for a few minutes," she insisted with a kind of innocence.

Using endearing words was one of the rules of the game that she had not yet fully mastered. A regular customer would almost consider her an amateur.

Torres sat down and gave her a quick once-over: average height, brown hair and eyes. She was not yet a hardened prostitute with grotesque features. A slight, ingenuous smile was her principal trait. Her age was somewhere between 18 and 19.

"Why did you come in here?"

"I came in for a snack."

"Nobody comes into this place just for a snack," she said, taking hold of one of his hands.

The boy, with a quick jerk, tried to free his hand, but she held it firmly.

"I can see that you're not a customer here maybe nowhere," her voice was softer now than at the beginning.

"I came in here for a snack, nothing else."

The contact with her hand repulsed him.

"Well, I can see that you're broke; your dinner was poor, but if, in fact, you didn't want anything from us, why did you look at us that way?"

"Me?!"

He was behaving like a typical yokel. After all, that's what he was. Lack of money made the physical act impossible and inhibited him, preventing him from assuming the look of an experienced man. He would have liked to leave as quickly as possible, but her holding his hand made it difficult.

"Business is pretty slow right now at seven o'clock. Would you like to sleep with me? You could pay me later..."

"I can't. I have to go to school. I'll come earlier tomorrow and maybe..."

"You'll come tomorrow?!" she exclaimed, interrupting him, delighted. "It would be good to get the money together. It's only 50 cruzeiros. If you want to, today, I could..."

"Tomorrow," he repeated hurriedly. "Well, see you then."

Torres withdraws his hand a little violently, gets up and is about to leave when she grabs his arm.

"Wait, I'll go to the corner with you."

The street had an atmosphere of mystery. Traffic at that hour was light. He had the impression that behind those walls and badly painted doors repugnant, animal-like creatures were hiding. Neon signs poorly lit frequented bars. Inside them, men could be found drinking brandy, down on their luck and life; their faces showing the misery of their souls.

"Don't think I'm like the others. I came from the country a month ago. I had run away with a man; he abandoned me, and here I am."

"Why didn't you get a job?"

"I could only get work as a domestic. I didn't want to work that hard, and I thought it would be easier to make money this way."

"And isn't it?"

"A little. I still don't have much experience. Don't you understand? I'd like to go with you, but I know that you're broke."

This confession hurt him. He had the urge to drag her away and enslave her as punishment for her callousness.

134

"If you want me, I won't charge you anything. You look like a boyfriend I had when I was 17. I almost married him. He liked me, but I liked other boys. I went out with him and with the others. I kissed, I embraced... Well, it doesn't matter. Will you really come tomorrow?"

"Yes, I will."

They walk slowly. Arriving at the corner, she doesn't stop and neither does he. They keep on walking.

"Do you like guavas?" she asked, taking on a childlike look.

"Yes, but how did you know that I'm from the country?"

"Your manner. Where do you come from?"

"Botucatu."

"Botucatu! I'm from Ribeirão Preto. Is Botucatu bigger?"

"It's smaller."

"Do you miss it?"

"A lot."

"I miss Ribeirão, too. The country is different, isn't it?"

"Yes, it is," he responded, a little more cheerful.

Shared feelings have brought them closer together.

"Come tomorrow, I won't charge you anything, just the room rent. No, you don't even have to pay for the room. Come at six o'clock. I'll wait for you in front of the bar," she said, elated.

"See you tomorrow, then."

"Until tomorrow."

Torres, taking long strides left her. He wanted to get away from there as quickly as possible.

His mind wandered during physics class.

Who's she sleeping with now? he asked himself. *What a sad life! She sells her body, she sells her soul, she sells her dignity. Man is a*

135

repulsive animal: he kills himself, he prostitutes himself, he hates himself and keeps on smiling. Aren't certain jobs a sort of prostitution? Sex like so many things, shouldn't be sold.

He feels pity for the social situation of the girl. *Without a doubt, girls like her deserve compassion instead of a reprimand. They suffer cruelty, disease and demoralization, all the worse things that can be offered to a human being. It may represent, by its cruelties, diseases and demoralization, one of the very worst things offered to a human being.* And it was with this profound feeling of pity that he remembered one of the parables of the Gospel: 'Let he who is without sin cast the first stone.' *How wonderful it is to see God himself absolve a prostitute! I'm going to look up that passage in the Bible tonight...*

Reading the Holy Book was a daily habit ever since he had experienced its impact at Mass. Every night, before going to sleep, he enjoyed great peacefulness from its teachings, and this practice kept the flame of his mysticism alive.

Back home, he leafed through the Bible, looking for that incident, and he found, starting in Chapter 7, verse 36 of the Gospel of St. Luke, the account of 'The Forgiven Sinner.'

What wisdom! he affirmed to the pillow. *But this isn't the parable of the first stone!* He turned a few more pages looking for it, but, exhausted by the day's events closed the book and fell asleep.

* * *

On the following Sunday, early in the morning, Torres received a telephone call from Sonia.

"Would you like to go with us to a dance this afternoon?"

The invitation disturbed him because he had so little money.

When we go out, we'll share the costs, he remembered Sonia had said on the train.

136

And what if she forgets? I don't have enough money even for the tickets. I can't risk it. It would be too humiliating. Hey, maybe my brother could loan me some! he encouraged himself.

But his brother was going through the same difficulties. He had begun to give private lessons, but the extra amounts that came in were spent immediately.

"Sonia, unfortunately I can't go with you," he said, chagrined.

"Is it because of the exams?"

"Yes, I have a lot to study."

"Why don't you study at night?"

"There's not enough time. I have to get a good grade in biology."

"All right," she said, somewhat disappointed, "if you change your mind, call me. My roommate and I will go alone. 'Bye.'"

"Goodbye," he answered, slamming down the phone. What did the poor telephone have to do with his unhappiness?

Damn! This is just too much!

His despair was so great, he felt like going out and stealing something as the only way out. His physical and moral debilitation were what led men to steal. He came to the conclusion that this vice is a problem of education and not one of necessity.

During lunch that Sunday, he ruminated over the execrable spaghetti about his misfortune.

If you change your mind..., he remembered. *But how can I change my mind?*

As the afternoon progressed, unhappiness and loneliness made him experience aversion to everything and everyone. Nothing seemed to be right. It was as if he were from another world, living these moments on earth. He carried these feelings to Church.

There the choir intoned Gregorian chants in fine tuned harmony, exuding etherealness and bliss. The soloist with an inspired and excellent voice, caught the peoples' attention for a few moments, and some heads turned to see who it was.

Torres joined in whole heartedly. As he began feeling more and more involved with the religious rites, his aversion began to disappear. That strange sensation of companionship again took hold of him.

The line to the confessional, just ahead of him, was short. He went over to it without quite knowing why. He confessed, he communed, and, as in previous times, he was reluctant to leave; the mystic environment relieved his despair. He felt comforted and as one with the structure of the temple. He feared leaving and re-encountering the anguish and loneliness of the afternoon. Outside it was night, the night of those ordinary dances in Botucatu and in São Paulo.

Lifting up his eyes, he sees above the empty altar an image of the crucified Jesus, and he smiles.

* * *

"Why did you smile?" interrupts Ruiz, astonished.

"It was a mystic and happy smile that sprang from within me, spontaneously. It was a total redemption of my being by those philosophic directives. I felt perfectly integrated with all they meant; I was one of them. And a silent and powerful message was transmitted from the crucified Christ:

There is nothing more beyond this...

138

"And it was then that I discovered the reason for the intense companionship: He had suffered to the ultimate degree, and I was sharing in His suffering."

* * *

After a while, Torres left the church and went home. The peace he assimilated in the church accompanied him all the way home.

I'm really not so alone, he thought.

Days later, on his way to school, he felt his arm being grabbed from behind and he turned around, startled.

"Why didn't you come?" asked the young girl he had met at the cheap restaurant.

"I couldn't. I had exams."

"But it was for free. I wasn't going to charge you anything!"

This fact, for her, should have convinced him to come.

"It wasn't possible."

"Come today, then. I still won't charge anything."

"No, I have exams again today."

"Rats! Exams, again!"

"At the end of the year we have exams every day," he explained, satisfied with the evasion.

"Can I walk with you to the corner?"

"Of course."

They walked a few slow steps. She tried to behave like a shy girl from the country. Her forced language and superficial manners showed her preoccupation in establishing a social relationship.

They passed the corner and continued talking without concern; she was hanging on to his arm.

"You look so much like my boyfriend from Ribeirão!"

"You already said that."

"But it's true, he was exactly like you!"

As she went on about her boyfriend, Torres studied her features. A full face, slightly turned up nose, sparkling eyes, but her disperse naivete continued to be her principal characteristic.

"Why don't you get out of this life and go back home?" he asked her without really understanding why he asked.

"I can't anymore. You know very well that I can't."

"Why not? You've only been here a short time, haven't you?"

"Yes, a month."

"Then put it all behind you while you can. Later on it will be difficult. After all, you haven't committed any crime."

"Well, no… I'm not really a criminal," she confirmed after much thought.

"Then if you don't feel like a criminal, get out of this life once and for all."

"Is it possible… oh! Forget it!"

They came to another corner and said goodbye. Torres noticed that she was daydreaming, chewing on some obscure thought. He turned his back, walked some twenty steps and turned around; the girl remained stock still, meditating.

She spotted him, gave a wave of her hand, turned and left.

The following day, Torres, overcome by a strange altruism, went to find her at the cheap restaurant.

"I haven't seen Rosa today," answered the waiter with a leer. "You have a date with her, don't you?"

"No, it's not what you're thinking," he added, surprised.

"And what might I be thinking?" the man protested, angry. "I'm not a pimp."

His solicitous face was replaced by a scowl. Picking up the glasses, he began to wash them violently. His frail body showed chronic fatigue, and his chapped hands betrayed a constant contact with dishwater.

"Hmpf! These boys..." he mumbled.

Torres, feeling humiliated, was about to leave.

"Hey, wait a minute. Do you happen to have a five spot, buddy?" his voice becoming pleasant.

"What for?"

"Well, buddy, if you could help me out, I might be able to help you out, too. But don't go thinking I'm a pimp," he added roughly. "That, I'm not; I'm just trying to help out for a little change," he completed, calmly.

"I don't have any money," he answered, moving in the direction of the door.

"Five! Boy, this guy is nuts!"

He spent half an hour walking around the block looking for Rosa. Now that he knew her name, it would be easier to find her.

"Rosa?" said a prostitute who was at the corner. "I don't know her, but won't I do?" she offered with a slight smile.

"No, you won't," he answered, naively.

"Beat it, sissy; who do you think you are? Who do you think I... Why you son of a... Get out of here and stop bothering me."

The boy was shook up, alarmed by the unexpected reaction. It dawned on him that in that district one couldn't ask anything. He walked around for another fifteen minutes but could find no trace of Rosa. Giving up on the search, he drank a cup of coffee in a bar and went to school.

The following day, he decided to find her at any cost. His awareness of having rejected Rosa overwhelmed him; he knew that he might be able to help her, and this relieved his loneliness. There existed for him, then, God, Sonia, Rosa and himself; so he decided to sacrifice his meager resources in order to find her.

"Two isn't enough," protested the waiter.

"It's all I have. I can't give you any more."

"Oh, I know. You have to 'pay' her," he concluded with that same leer. "All right, I'll take the two bills. Hand 'em over.'"

"Hand over what?"

"The two bills, or did you think I would tell you where she is before getting them. You really are new at this!"

Torres opened his wallet, took out two Cruzeiros, and paid him.

The waiter took a greasy notebook from his pocket, ran his finger down the alphabet and stopped at 'R.'

"Rosa, here it is. She's on this same street, number 601."

"Thank you."

"If you want, I've got a new young blonde who's a real knockout. For you, I'll let you have her address for only three Cruzeiros."

"Not now. Goodbye."

"Don't forget, if you need any other information, look me up. I have files on all of them: blondes, brunettes, red-heads, even..."

The boy hurried out without hearing the end.

I'll be damned if that miserable heel isn't a pimp.

"Rosa isn't here. Would you like someone else?" asked the woman who answered the door.

"Someone else? No, I want to talk to Rosa."

"Ah, you only like her, then. You're a child to fall so easily. You should choose another."

"No thanks," he said, crisply.

"All right, no need to get upset. She went to the post office, and I guess she picked up some guy."

"I'll come by again, tomorrow. Tell her to wait for me."

"As you wish, but what a crush!"

He looked for her the next day, but no Rosa. The end of that week was also the end of that month. Monday would bring the money for December. It would be another month of sacrifices. He had stumbled through the month of November, and the effects of his forced economies were making themselves felt: he was thin and exhausted.

During the week, aside from the extravagance of the two cruzeiros, Torres had saved a good amount. This had been accomplished with a view to a Sunday with Sonia. But it was only enough to pay for his own ticket, and he felt obliged to think of a way to remind her of that. *When we go out, it'll be Dutch treat.*

"Sonia," he said on the telephone, "would you like to go out with me, today?"

"Yes, we can," she answered happily. "The dance on Sunday was wonderful. Shall we go again?"

"Yes, but only if it's Dutch treat."

He had rehearsed it so much that he just blurted it out.

"Dutch treat?!"

"Well, you know, Sonia, I don't have enough money," he explained bashfully.

"Oh! Yes, you're right. Of course it'll be Dutch treat."

"At three o'clock. All right?"

"OK."

* * *

"How nice it is to dance with you, again. It's been three months, hasn't it?"

He was making an effort to dance well, and the sweeps around the dance floor were light as air. Sonia was a little distracted as though looking for someone.

"Dance a little with Miriam," she asked him as a favor.

Miriam was her plain, skin-and-bones friend. Up to that moment, she hadn't yet had a dance. There wasn't a man attracted enough to ask her.

Torres started dancing with her and saw someone else ask Sonia to dance. He did his best to catch up with her and, when he saw her, gave her a broad smile. She returned his smile a little austerely; his affection, however, forgave her.

Sonia's dancing partner must have been an old friend. The constant laughter and dialog made it obvious that he was not a recent acquaintance.

"Who's dancing with Sonia?" he asked, jealously, dragging Miriam around after her girl friend.

"That boy danced with her last Sunday."

So that's who she was looking for!

"Is there something between them?"

The question was asked a little harshly. Torres was already tired of the 'walking skeleton,' and his anger with Sonia was directed toward Miriam.

"Sonia told me about him during the week. It seems he's a medical student."

144

"Oh! So what?"

When the music had ended, the four of them met in a corner of the dance hall. Sonia introduced Torres to the young man.

"A friend from the country," she said, pointing to him.

"Pleased to meet you," said the boy.

"Shall we have a soda?" asked the girl, adroitly. She wanted to keep the boy at her side.

They went on ahead, and it was up to Torres, farther back, to escort the little shrew of a partner.

A friend from the country, he could still hear the phrase. *So much sacrifice for nothing.*

At the table, Miriam took over and, propped up on her elbows, kept him from approaching Sonia. This approach, however, might have been ineffective anyhow; she was 'putty' in the hands of the medical student.

How beautiful she is! he observed, frustrated.

His growing uneasiness drove him to dislike being together with the three of them. And so the time passed at the dance.

They said good bye at the door of the boarding house, and Sonia, all smiles now, thanked him for the outing.

"Why don't all four of us go out again next Sunday?"

The medical student accepted. They looked at Torres for his answer.

"I can't. I have exams..."

And so ended his dreamed-of Sunday.

On the following day, Torres received the thousand monthly cruzeiros; he paid for the preparatory course and the high school as quickly as possible. When he had the receipt in his hand, he felt that the high school diploma was assured, but another month of belt tightening awaited him. His biggest problem, however, was Sonia; he couldn't get her out of his mind.

Despite his distraction with Sonia he remembered Rosa. He knew he could be of help to her and set out to look for her. He decided to investigate her strange disappearance early in the morning when all the prostitutes were still at home, re-composing themselves for the next night's activities.

The street that morning was calm; there was practically no-one on the corners. A few passersby showed the effects of the previous night's revelry on their faces. He walked back and forth in front of number 601 several times; he couldn't summon up the courage to knock. After a while he planted himself on the doorstep hoping to hear some sign of movement within the house. The scraping of chairs alerted him. He knocked. The landlady sleepily answered the door in her nightgown.

"You again! And at this hour?!"

"Hasn't she come yet? I think it's strange..."

"Hold on..." she interrupted him. "Rosa came back yesterday afternoon."

"Then she's here?"

"No, she packed up her things and left. I always thought that girl wasn't cut out for this."

"Went where?" he inquired, worried; he felt responsible for her.

"I don't know. She told another girl that she had a job."

"A job. Oh, now I see!"

"See what?" she asked, irritated.

"Oh, nothing. Thank you," he said, leaving in a hurry.

"Wait! I want to know just what's going on. I don't like it when they take my girls out of here," she shouted in protest.

146

"Be seeing you," he answered from a distance. His previous experience had warned him of possible outbursts.

"Don't you come around here, again, you hear? Go to... you wretched dog," she cursed at him, slamming the door after him.

Striding away, he was thinking.

Employed? That's good! But why am I acting this way?

* * *

"I went to find part of the answer at mass the next Sunday," he says to Ruiz. "When I saw her for the first time, I saw only the sordid aspect of her life; I hadn't comprehended the fact that, under that mask, there was a soul."

"And how did you discover the existence of that soul?" asks Ruiz with interest.

"The description that she had given of her past and her indecision when I raised the possibility of her returning to Ribeirão Preto showed me that here was an opportunity to save a sout that I couldn't miss. If I had wanted to save something, it certainly was not her body."

"And why did you want to save it?"

"Today I can give you an answer to that question, but on that Sunday I couldn't. I hoped that she would change her life, and I felt good just kneeling in that Church; two big mysteries for me."

* * *

Mass continued as usual. Now and then Torres was surprised to find himself observing the appearance of the people sharing the pew with him. At communion, he prayed for Rosa to find peace of spirit and realized for the first time that his life had some purpose.

147

When the religious service was over, he felt the need to release some of the warm happiness that he felt and ardently wished to share with someone.

Wandering around, he suddenly found himself at the door of a club. They were holding an afternoon dance; entrance cost five cruzeiros, and he had six. That amount had been destined for a more hearty dinner. The wretched lunch at the boarding house had been intolerable that day, and his stomach was resonating with a music quite different from what his ears were hearing from the ballroom.

A battle of sounds was then engaged between his stomach and the trumpets. He was being entranced, like a cobra by a flute, but the digestive organ, sensing imminent defeat, restrained the legs that would have taken him to the ticket window. It was black and humiliating hunger that won the roll of the dice.

* * *

"Man is nothing more than a being in conflict," interrupts Ruiz, wanting to round off the young man's narrative. "This conflict develops between rationality and irrationality. The psyche on one side against animal instincts on the other. The desire of food is a strong ally of the latter."

* * *

Torres' legs ended up taking him far away from that place of pleasure. At last, he was going to have dinner. The ebullient, bombastic discourse of the stomach had triumphed... but not convinced. His head continuously looked back, and, as he was about to turn the corner out of sight of the club, he stopped and remained still in the same position for a few minutes, then resolutely went back. The psyche had won after all.

He danced as never before, but the end came all too quickly. Upon leaving the club, however, hunger charged a heavy price for its defeat.

He went to a corner bar; his eyes, windows for that noisy organ of his stomach reveled at the sight of little cakes, flaky pastries, and all the other goodies provocatively displayed. To him they were now as intangible as nectar on Olympus. He ordered a French roll with butter and left, feeling himself reduced to the smallest measure of importance.

Upon seeing himself surrounded by pedestrians, he noted the effects of his upbringing insofar as perishable and transformable matter was concerned. He felt, then, that there was something very wrong with all of that, and that the human beings around him should lend him a helping hand because he was one of them.

As he passed by the side of the Church where he had been only a few hours ago, he remembered that there existed a God, a God-Man who had fasted forty days and had been a spirit in the flesh. He broke out in a smile and understood, in that moment, that he was nothing if not a spirit that had not come from nothing and would not go back to being nothing. He was imperishable and would come to rest in Him. Therefore, for his happiness, it was his spirit that he should nourish.

Soon afterward he felt revulsion for the selfishness of his life; he also had not looked around him. Therefore, he decided that his existence would have the sum total of good actions as its purpose.

But what good actions could I perform? Rosa?!

He woke up the next morning thinking of Sonia... he longed for her and felt sad, which proved his feelings concerning her. He made an effort to forget her, and Rosa took her place. Not the prostitute Rosa but the domestic employee

Rosa, and a pleasant sensation of triumph ran through his body. The two alternatives balanced each other, and the day passed as monotonously as any other.

In the late afternoon, he walked through the red light district when he felt a tug on his arm.

"Hey, wait up. How have you been?"

"Rosa, you here!" he said, happily. "Where have you been? I've been looking for you these past few days."

"Let's walk," she answered, pushing him lightly forward, "I don't want to stay on this street a moment longer than I have to."

"But tell me, where have you been these days?"

"You remember when you told me that I had only been here a short time, and that I should go back home while I could?" she asked, stammering.

"I remember."

"I thought a lot about it, and I thought that since I had committed no crime I could go back."

"And so?"

"After I left you, I locked myself in my room, and when the landlady knocked on my door as time to go to work, I said I was in my monthly period. You know, don't you?"

"Yes, I know. Go on."

"I stayed in my room, and the following day I looked up the house that had advertised for a maid."

"And did you find it ok?"

"I'm a kitchen servant at a boarding house in Higieno-polis."

"And today? What are you doing here?"

"I only came back here to get my things. Wait. I'm mixing everything up. I haven't finished what I was going to say."

"Then say it."

They walked without noticing that they had passed the high school.

Now and then Torres was surprised to find himself observing her. The eyes were no longer puffy, her hair was well combed, and her clean, print dress made her face light up in a mixture of purity and happiness.

"I wrote a letter home asking if I could go back there. I received the answer today."

"What did the letter say?"

"My mother says that she cried a lot, and that my father won't be angry when I return."

"Just that?"

"No, she also said that my father has stopped drinking and gambling, and that he got a job as a truck driver."

"How wonderful!"

"She wants me to come back to help take care of the boys."

"And you're going back, aren't you?"

"Do you think I should?"

"But of course!"

"Oh, she also asked if I was expecting a baby."

"Are you?" he asked, alarmed.

"No, but she said I should come back even if I were, that she would find a way to raise it."

"Are you happy?"

"Very, but should I really go back? People will talk..."

"Now... what are they going to say?" he stuttered. "Well, they're not going to say anything."

"You think not?"

"If they say anything, don't pay any attention. It's much better there than here, don't you think?"

"Oh yes! Here it's just too horrible. So you think it won't matter."

"No. Well, it's already class time. I have to go."

"Already? I wanted to say goodbye to you."

"Then let's say goodbye now."

"Not here. You were good to me, and I want to thank you by going to bed with you..."

"What for? Now you'll never have to do that again with anyone," he said, astonished.

Torres reached the conclusion that Rosa's remorse was based entirely on professionalism. He lacked the knowledge and the eloquence to instill morality in the girl and couldn't, for that very reason, explain to her the motivation for physical purity. The desire to perform her profession well was still a little strange to him, but since he had felt those first positive emotions towards her at mass, these revelations no longer surprised him.

"Where is your boarding house? I'll have lunch there tomorrow."

"Wonderful!" she euphorically exclaimed.

She gave him the address, and they said goodbye. Torres walked a few steps away and looked back; she had waited for him so as to give a wave of her hand. He walked a little farther and, turning around once again, saw her turn right at the corner. Rosa no longer belonged to that street.

His studies at the high school were going well. The exams in which he needed the highest grades had already been taken; the diploma was a sure thing. His improvement in the preparatory course continued to increase, but he still had a long way to go to be considered a good student.

His physical shape remained stable without getting any thinner; his morale, however, grew. He realized, now, that he no longer was adrift. Rosa and Sonia dominated him in different ways, causing his loneliness to decrease.

The following day, he had lunch at the boarding house where Rosa worked. He ate like he hadn't eaten for some time.

Throughout the entire meal she hovered about the boy, and some curious glances were thrown his way; this curiosity came from the student boarders.

"Did you have enough?" Rosa asked him, letting her exaggerated attention show through.

"Quite."

"Could I talk with you a little later? I get off at two and have to return only at four."

"All right," he would be incapable of denying her any request. His full stomach put him in debt to her.

Her face held a beautiful expression: it was the peace given to those beings who have fulfilled themselves. He paid for the meal and said goodbye.

Torres went for a walk in the neighborhood and was reminded of Sonia; he wanted more than ever to be at her side. That medical student had deeply wounded his self-esteem.

He had dreamed, ever since that Sunday, of a new opportunity to tell her of his affection. If her reception were negative, he would abandon the pursuit. And it was with that purpose in mind that he headed for a telephone booth; he wanted to try out his last hopes.

"Sonia?"

"Yes, who is it?"

He answered with a stammer and finished, "I... I wanted to know if... if I might have any hope at all with you."

"With me? But why do you ask? What do you mean by that?"

"Well, I think that... I like you"

"Me?"

"Yes, for some time."

"What a great surprise!"

"Are you still dating that boy?"

"Yes, I am."

"Is it definitive?"

"It's a little early to say."

"Because if it isn't definitive, maybe I might have some hope?"

"Really, I don't know what to say," she answered with embarrassment.

"Tell me straight out, Sonia. It's very important to me."

"Look, can't we go into this some other time?"

"I need an answer right now."

"I've always thought of you as a good friend."

"Nothing more?"

"I don't think so."

"Thank you and... farewell."

"Farewell... but why?"

"I want to forget you, and it would be too difficult if we continued to see each other."

"Wait, don't be so hasty. Maybe..."

He heard nothing more; a lump in his throat kept him from saying goodbye, and so he carelessly hung up the telephone.

He left the telephone booth miserably depressed. His personality had always demanded quick resolutions, and it was with a 'yes or no' that he had closed off this last hope.

I will forget her, I will forget her, no matter the cost.

He walked about a bit more and, at two o'clock, went to meet Rosa at the door of the boarding house. She arrived ten minutes later. She had put on her makeup with care; her dress, the same as on the previous day, had been neatly pressed; her brushed hair fell to her shoulders, and her happy face made her attractive. It was difficult to compare her now to the slut of a few days ago.

They took a bus and got off at Ibirapuera Park.

"I'm only going home at the end of the month," she explained.

"I thought you'd go sooner."

"I can't go home with empty hands. As soon as I receive my pay, I'll buy a few presents and be on my way."

"There's no danger of your feeling regrets? I wish you would go right away."

"You want to be rid of me?"

"That's not it."

He couldn't tell her that as long as she was there, he felt morally responsible for her; her departure would represent a relief for his conscience.

"Let's go back to the subject of yesterday: you don't have to sleep with anyone anymore."

"Never again?"

"Well... only when you marry."

Torres didn't understand Rosa's concept of morality. In this respect she acted with a strange naturalness.

"Some of the students are flirting with me. I don't see any harm in sleeping with them once in awhile."

"Then why did you get off the street?" he asked, enraged.

"There it's different, they take advantage of you, they even hit you."

"Weren't you taught how to act decently?"

"What do you mean, decently?"

"Not to sleep with anyone."

"Oh! My mother told me to have a baby only when I got married."

"Just that?! How were you raised?"

They sat on one of the park benches in front of the lake. Some boats slid smoothly across the water.

"My father drank a lot, and my mother had to work outside. I was the eldest, and I had to take care of my two little brothers and the house."

"Didn't you go to school?"

"Just for three years. After that I couldn't go anymore."

"And in Church, didn't anybody teach you anything?"

"No, I never went to Church."

"Then when was it that you..." he interrupted, not knowing how to broach the subject of the loss of her virginity, "that you slept with someone for the first time?" he finished, lamely.

"It was three years ago, when I was 15. My father brought some friends home, and they were also friends of my mother, and they were horsing around with her and with me..."

"Horsing around how?"

"Well, you know... It was one of these friends that I ran away with. He told me he would give me new clothes and presents, but wound up dumping me here."

And just how am I going to instill any morals into that empty head?

"Rosa, do you believe in God?"

"I never really thought about it, but I heard that sleeping with someone without being married is a sin."

"Yes, it is."

"Then my mother is always sinning."

"Rosa, your mother...," he was very embarrassed, "There exists someone, a God, who says: 'Sin not against chastity.' Do you know what that is?"

"No!"

"That you can't sleep with anyone."

"But my mother..."

"Your mother... she didn't know that it was a sin, she really didn't," he stated, satisfied with the idea that was being born, "but now that I have explained it to you, you can no longer act like this. Rosa, the commandments of the church are..."

* * *

From that day forward he let himself be dominated by the apostolic feeling that was growing within him. He was not prepared for these activities and for that reason started to read the Bible with greater frequency and memorize the catechism. Imbued with these concepts, he eagerly continued teaching Rosa. He wanted to transform her into a religious person as quickly as possible, and the desire to do the right thing and instill Christian morality made him very happy.

The effects of these efforts made everything else seem secondary. His study time diminished and his situation in the preparatory course began to deteriorate. The entrance exam for engineering would be given in two months and, now, he couldn't care less.

The high school had already given him his diploma with excellent references. The grades imprinted in his report card at the end of the course showed a remarkable improvement.

His disillusion with Sonia diminished as far as it could, and loneliness his had ended completely. He was no longer alone. Rosa and religion absorbed him.

Christmas came in a rush, and with the end of the year came the departure of Rosa. She didn't want to leave him and only decided to go at his insistence. On seeing her depart, Torres felt a great relief in the satisfaction of a duty fulfilled.

The joy he felt for having elevated the morals of Rosa was quite different from anything that he had ever felt up to that moment. His pure and useful life placed upon his lips that happy smile that can only be found in the mystics. And so as not to lose that happiness, he began to go to communion daily.

There is nothing more than this, he remembered from the message of Jesus to him every time he beheld Jesus crucified before his eyes.

This succession of events left him more confused than ever as to his future profession. A clear directive for his destiny was very difficult for him at that moment. And it was with this feeling of doubt that he took the exams for the course in engineering.

He had to repeat the exams. If that had happened to him a while ago, it would be cause for lamentations, cursing his teachers and their methods, and a whole series of improprieties. Now he felt a great consolation; engineering no longer meant anything to him. He had decided, after this failure, that he would be the author of his own destiny.

158

What am I to be, then? He pondered. *I'm not interested in either law or medicine.*

* * *

"Was that when you entered the seminary?" interrupts Ruiz.

"The right opportunity had not yet arisen for a proper analysis of what I had gone through in São Paulo. That would happen days later, but before that day had arrived..."

* * *

He presented himself to his parents defeated and confused. Their shock was great; their sacrifices had been useless. Disillusioned, they laid out new plans, but he opposed them all. Torres wanted to think, just think.

"What meaning is there in all those masses that I took part in and in Rosa?" he asked Brother Paul, a Franciscan monk who had exercised some influence over him in his youth; his advice, however, was more often the cause of ridicule by him and his friends. They were, at that time, the saviors of the world, the "know-it-alls".

"Why don't you go on the retreat I am going to give in Barueri at carnival time?" he asked. "It's quite possible that you'll find your answer there."

Pauls appearance, the thin beard, the Franciscan habit, the sandals, all idealized by the saint who gave his name to the order, still disturbed him.

"It's an opportunity you should not miss; everything that you have experienced may have some meaning," insisted the priest on seeing the boy's indecision.

He went.

The location was appropriate for retreats. The main building, a modern, rectangular edifice, was situated on top of a hill. Seated in a lounge chair on the terrace, one could see a lake with geese, ducks, and boats in an anchorage just below; green grass surrounded it, and flowers of many colors bloomed all over. To the left there was a sports area: parallel bars, hoops, basketball and volley courts. To the right was the home of the little sisters who took care of the place. The diminutive suited them well; they were not tall and their constant smiling captivated and endeared them to all.

Torres fit into the place easily. He and nine other boys would get up early in the morning and meditate while walking on the dew covered grass and watch the sun come up in a way that was different from what they were used to seeing. The priest led them in thanking God for such beautiful moments. From there they would go to the chapel to attend Mass; the ceremony took place in rustic humility. He and his companions placed the cloth upon the table, the chalice, the wine, the water and the missal. They all surrounded it under the radiant look of the crucifix and assisted in the recitation of the religious office and liturgy.

Torres felt deeply envious of the priest at the time of the elevation. He ardently wanted to hold Christ in his own hands and, when he communed, he wanted to receive Him in His plenitude. The strange feelings that he had experienced on those occasions in São Paulo grew within him.

After mass, they had breakfast in silence. The retreat was a closed one and they were prohibited from speaking, but the looks that they exchanged were happy ones.

Breakfast finished, they went into the conference room. It was there that they received the teachings appropriate to that phase of life, where indecision struggled with certainty. Everything, then, was very right for him, very impressive.

160

When the lecture was over, he had lunch and went to his room called a "cell". There he began to meditate on the matter discussed at the conference.

In the afternoon, another talk was followed by coffee and cookies and, following that, he said the rosary while walking through the garden. This prayer reflected the beauty of his religion, which blossomed forth in all its grandeur in his soul. Peace was mirrored in his face. Torres was totally happy.

At dusk, he had some free time. He would go to the lake, sit on one of the benches and watch the sun go down in a demonstration of beauty he had never experienced before. The little sisters walked through the garden; they would smile and he would smile back.

He had supper, said the prayers proper to the nocturnal period, went to his cell to jot down impressions and resolutions, and slept.

... Eight years later, Torres finished the seminary.

* * *

"The reasons that led you into the priesthood are quite well defined in your story. But I think your personality forced you into definitive decisions even though there is nothing in nature that is definitive and permanent. Your disappointment with Sonia was quite vivid when you decided to become a priest. Rosa, another reason, showed you the satisfaction that comes from disinterested altruism. Also, your loneliness and inability to adapt to life in the capital led you to an encounter with God. No-one can live completely alone; in extreme cases, one takes himself as a companion and talks to himself or unites with God. Your revelations prove the utility of the test that you yourself proposed," continues Ruiz. "Your story shows that you must convince yourself with

161

stronger reasons than these that you have presented; only then will you be completely certain of your priestly vocation."

The lounge chairs, where Torres and Ruiz had accommodated themselves after dinner, squeaked as they got up.

"Well, I'm going to bed. Are you going to stay here?"

"I'm going to the bar; then I'll be down shortly," Torres answers.

They part; the clock on the deck marks 2300 hours.

The boy goes to the bar, sits down at a corner table, and orders a martini. Movement at that hour is very light; the ship's night club has attracted some young people by the romanticism of music heard in the half-light.

Torres meditates and his face reflects all of the drama of those moments. Odete had demanded an answer for the morning of the following day, and the possibilities still seem far too equal to him.

After a while, the waiter announces the closing of the bar. The young man looks at the clock with surprise and sees that it's three o'clock.

He goes down to the cabin, undresses and puts on his pajamas, climbs up into his berth and turns to the porthole. The moon reflects in a shimmering layer of silver on the sea.

Chapter IX

Some days later...

Croma had docked quite early and would only leave at nightfall. The passengers, therefore, had the opportunity to become acquainted with the famous French port of Cannes. Torres, Odete and her mother Maria were returning from a stroll through the business district.

"Wouldn't you like to have lunch on land?" asks Odete's mother. "The food on board is becoming unbearable."

"You're quite right," he answers, amiably.

The restaurant they choose, the Chez les Pecheurs, is located near the dock.

"I'm glad you think the same way I do. When we left Barcelona, I swore that I would eat on land in the next port. Now what I don't understand is why this girl prefers to eat on board!" she concludes, looking at her with curiosity.

"I've already told you, mother, that I see no reason to spend money needlessly," says Odete a little waspishly.

"How you've changed my daughter! She always liked regional dishes, and now that we're here, all she talks about is economizing! And that's not all," she says, turning to the young man, "I think it strange that she, being so liberal, refused to buy those summer clothes in the Rue d'Antibes."

"Perhaps she doesn't need any clothes," he comments naively.

"That's no reason! And what about the perfumes? She always liked perfumes, and French ones, too! Now that we're here at their source she doesn't want to buy them. I think the Mediterranean air isn't doing her any good."

"Oh, mother, it's a long voyage, and there'll be no lack of opportunities; and why buy more things when I've already bought some Caleche glass in the ship's store?"

"Very well, you don't need to get upset, I was only curious," she apologizes as the waiter serves her whitefish with scallops cooked in garlic, saffron and olive oil.

Odete's mother, when she chose that dish, insisted on informing the waiter of all the details printed on the menu as though the dish were new to him.

The restaurant, despite being on the Quai des Docks, surrounded by bars and sailors' boardinghouses, is decorated in good taste and well frequented. It's exotic menu, specializing in seafood, attracts tourists who spend their holidays on the Cote d'Azur.

"Mother, returning to that subject of early this morning, why didn't you want to join the busload of passengers who are going to Nice and Monte Carlo?" demands Odete.

"I've already told you that these excursions need to made in the company of someone. If I have to go alone, I prefer to remain on board ship."

"Dr. Ruiz told me this morning that he's going on the trip, and if you like, I could ask him to accompany you."

"But the two of you really aren't going? It's such a nice opportunity that..."

"Don't insist, mother. We want to go to the Lerin Islands."

164

"All right," she finally agrees, "Dr. Ruiz' company would be pleasant."

"Would you like some more wine?" offers Torres, noticing her empty glass.

"Just a little more. This white wine... what's it called?"

"Escarene."

"Ah, Escarene. It's very good."

The waiter clears away the dishes and then serves cheese with torte. Odete's mother, at the suggestion of the young man, tries a piece of Sospel, a cheese made from goat's milk.

"How I miss Lisbon," she says. "It's a beautiful city! You remember..."

They finish dessert and coffee, and with it Maria's impressions of Lisbon. Most certainly, if there had been more time, the monologue would have gone on interminably.

* * *

Torres waits for Odete on the quarter deck from where he can see some of the frenetic movement in the bay. The Cote d'Azur is at the height of the tourist season, and on the sunlit bay where the Croma is anchored, sailboats and yachts from ports everywhere outnumber the fishing boats.

Just in front of the ship, dominating the view from the deck, are the luxury hotels along the Croisette. The Municipal Casino, triangular in shape, is located at the end of this beach, in front of the Quai St. Pierre, where the fishermen stretch out their nets to dry.

The young man remembers, while taking in the views, that he had left Lisbon three days ago. The emotions that he had felt upon arriving in the Portuguese capital after ten days on the open sea were not the same as when they later arrived in Barcelona. Since the Spanish port had not been their first stop, it had become just another routine occurrence on the voyage for him.

But now, together with the other passengers crowding the deck, he was excited with the sight of Cannes and with the constant announcements from the loudspeaker. The excursion to the Lerin Islands would leave in 15 minutes, and Odete had not yet arrived.

Torres stepped back from the railing, worried. Some girls standing behind him rush to fill the empty place that he had vacated and shove him closer to the main gangplank. She arrives shortly after.

They greet each other and rush off with hands intertwined to the Ufficio del Commissario where the group for the Lerin Islands is to meet. Accustomed to the passengers' normal noisiness, they are surprised by the quiet chattering of the other tourists. They are 15 in all, nearly all older persons who have already seen Nice and Monte Carlo and are now looking for a rest on the tranquil islands.

Maria and Dr. Ruiz have already left for Monaco. And only with their departure does the couple realize that they have been able to get away on the tour alone.

"I began to fear that my mother would go with us," she sighs, hanging on to the young man's arm.

"Her company isn't so disagreeable."

"You're just saying that to be nice; you were of a different opinion in Barcelona, remember?"

"You onght to understand that your mother's loneliness is terrible. I'm sorry now that I wanted to go to the bullfights without her. Do you remember her enthusiasm?"

"Just like always, when it comes to doing the right thing, you always prefer it, and I'm not a good daughter," she adds, faking sadness and then smiling afterward.

The launch draws up to the ship. They climb aboard and, 15 minutes later, having crossed the channel, they land on the island of Ste. Marguerite.

* * *

The couple walks hand in hand along the narrow road that crosses the island. Beautiful pine and eucalyptus woods invite them to rest, but curiosity about the unknown leads them to crossover to the other side.

Tired of walking, they sit in a clearing surrounded by pine trees on the opposite side from the anchorage; the sea, just in front of them, laps in little waves.

Odete sits leaning on the palm of her hand on the grass. Torres lies down, resting his head in her lap.

They do not speak. The girl looks at the calm sea; her appearance reveals worry and accumulated affection which is about to come to the surface. He, gazing up at her, says nothing. His attention is centered on the explanation he must soon give to his superior in Rome.

After a bit, she begins to run her fingers fondly through his hair.

"I think we should talk about our future," she says seriously.

"Yes, we should," Torres agrees, distractedly.

"The quickness with which all this has happened surprises me. 15 days ago, we hadn't even met, and now we're making plans for a future together just as natural as can be."

"And is that all that bad?"

"Not at all. What scares me, though, is the hand of destiny in all of this. If I hadn't asked you 'Italy?', remember..."

"How can I forget?!"

"... maybe we wouldn't be here looking at, so to speak, a a project for two."

"These days that we have spent together have made me see just how wrong I was. I am grateful to you for that. Most certainly, if I had decided to take my final vows and be ordained, I would have made a terrible priest."

She does not say anything. A seagull, mewling over the sea, draws her attention. The neck of the bird, extended downward, searches for the fish that guarantees its survival.

Torres follows Odete's look and remembers when he boarded the ship. The conviction that he had felt that day had been strong, but now, after his experiences aboard the Croma, he can see that life held certain illusions that, when discovered, were far from ideal.

"What I like in you now is seeing you so confident."

"And because I'm no longer indecisive," he affirms with conviction.

"That's true..."

"As I told you in Barcelona, I won't be able to accompany you on your trip through Europe. I don't have the money for it, and I won't allow you, under any circumstances, to loan it to me."

"You're very stubborn. I already told you that we would make you a kind of loan, and you could repay it in the future," she explains gently.

"No, while I'm at the Brazilian Pius Seminary in Rome, making my explanations, you two will make your tour of Europe, and we'll meet later in São Paulo. It's the best solution."

"If you go back to Brazil, I will, too."

"And what about your mother? What would she say about that? She's not going to want to miss the rest of her trip on our account!"

Odete can see the impossibility of arguing against Torres' convictions, but realizing that she still has two days to convince him, wants to calmly take advantage of those moments on the island.

"There was a time in my life," she says, changing the subject, "and I think it was when my father left us, that I thought I would never be happy again. I wanted to run away, hide from everything and everyone; nothing made any sense any more. Today, however, I feel as though I've been walking on air."

The curls of her hair falling about her shoulders and the emotion of these revelations give her appearance a certain serenity, making her look younger and prettier.

"You also deserve the credit for transforming my mother; it was very hard to convince her to go with Dr. Ruiz," she finishes with a smile.

"Do you remember Barcelona? The enthusiasm with which she walked from shop to shop gave her the look of an 18 year old."

They laugh together and feel even closer.

"How beautiful this place is!" comments Odete, looking at the pines on either side. "I think that men should share their growth with the plants and their perception with the animals so they don't risk becoming only a half-being."

"And to think that places like this are destroyed by building cities!"

"You're right. There are people in São Paulo, for example, who live for months, even years, without seeing the green of the fields. And, being unused to seeing them, when they come across a colorful countryside, they feel instinctively that there is something missing in their lives; it's the allure of their origins.

A murmur interrupts their reverie and they look behind them. A group of ten people is walking behind a French guide who gestures continually, trying to overcome the difficulties of the language barrier.

"Shall we go with them?" proposes Odete, getting up.

Joining the group, they fall in step with the others.

"As I have already said, Ste. Marguerite is three kilometers long and nine hundred meters wide. We have now reached the other side of the island," explains the guide in a mixture of Spanish and French, "or nine hundred meters from where we started out."

Pausing for a moment, he stops next to some boulders, takes a deep breath, and continues:

"The castle that we will see shortly... Oh, look, there it is," he indicates, walking toward it, "a medieval fortress. In the twelfth century, the celebrated Man in the Iron Mask was held prisoner there. General Bazaine, perhaps not as well known to you, was also one of its prisoners."

The tourists comment and exchange impressions among themselves. The guide, from the almost daily effort of repeating the same phrases, shows both physical and verbal fatigue.

"The island of Ste. Honorat is smaller; it is 1,500 meters long and 400 meters wide," he explains after a bit, pointing at it. "To the south is constructed an ancient fortified monastery and, to the north, there is another, modern one occupied by the Cistercian monks; entry is forbidden to women."

"What order is that?" asks one of the women.

The guide turns toward her, ready to answer; his demeanor reveals an extensive knowledge.

"It's an abbey of the order of St. Bernard, belonging to Cister, a famous monastery in Portugal."

On resuming their walk among the woods, Odete holds Torres' hand and whispers in his ear:

"Shall we stay a little longer here?"

"And the return? We shouldn't get so far away from the group."

"Nonsense, we still have two hours left!"

The young man agrees and they sit against a pine tree, their backs to the sea. He puts his arm around her and she nestles into his shoulder.

"Tired?" he asks, seeing her close her eyes.

"Happy," she responds, smiling. "I'm contemplating the happiness of this day."

"I feel happy too."

Torres runs his hand through Odete's hair in a caress. It's an almost unconscious gesture and reflects the feeling that has taken hold of him.

They grow quiet for there are no words to express these feelings. A simple touch and a simple loving look are sufficient to provide the happy everlastingness that passes through their spirits.

He, intoxicated by it all, holds her in a loving embrace and their lips meet in a long kiss. Nothing else exists then except Odete and their surroundings.

The moments that follow flood them with an intense joy of living. Oaths of love and fidelity are exchanged and their looks in these moments reflect not only love but also a nearly uncontrollable passion.

Two hours later, with the sunset, the launch crosses the strait quickly while they say goodbye to an already unforgettable Ste. Marguerite.

Arriving at the ship, Odete goes down to her cabin and the young man remains on deck, admiring the view of the city.

Cannes gradually grows dark, its sun reddened contours reveal the beauty of its architecture. The lights along the famous tree-lined Croisette are lit and in front of it the frothy waves on the beach turn silver with the reflected brightness.

He can still see what seemed to him to be the Festival Palace. When he had been there that morning, Odete had called his attention to the flowers and coconut palms planted along its sidewalks. He also recalls their walks through the steep little streets with arcades in the old city. In a short while, he can only distinguish the tower that presides over the beach. Cannes is covered with light.

Suddenly, as though he had been shaken by strong hands, he remembers the warnings of Ruiz.

* * *

"Don't make any definitive resolutions now. Your vocation may be your reason for living. The years in the seminary will compel you to meditate a lot and with greater intensity."

"I'm quite confident about this," declares the young man with conviction.

"But don't you see that you're being hasty?"

Torres faces the other way and doesn't answer.

"This is your main defect: for you it's all or nothing. Remember what I told you a few days ago: nothing in life is truly definitive."

"And what would you have me do, then? I can't continue with this indecision much longer. My feelings, why not say love, for Odete are sufficiently strong for me to decide in her favor. Nothing can change that now."

172

"Your conviction is an indisputable fact."

"And isn't that proof of the correctness of my decision?" he asks impatiently.

"Perhaps, but it may also represent a somewhat extreme endeavor, contrary to your conscience."

"I don't understand!"

"I mean that maybe you are forcing this decision upon yourself. The motives that have induced you can be explained by the emotions produced by the feminine contact that you have been unaccustomed to and by the fear of making Odete suffer a deception. These facts alone are enough to blind you to logical reasoning."

They are silent for a few moments, but in a moment the doctor resumes speaking.

"I intended, at the start of the voyage, only to put you in doubt as to your ecclesiastic vocation. Depending on developments, we could make a decision, possibly almost definitive, but never categorical. I advise you now to put everything on hold and consult during the next our months with the wise counselors of your religion."

The young man hesitates; the considerations of Ruiz have made him think.

"But, if you remember, she demanded a definition!"

"Yes," he agrees and, not wishing to interrupt him, lets him continue.

"I considered the pros and cons and came to the conclusion that the act of giving up the priesthood would not drive me away from God."

"I reiterate, it's too little time for such certainty. There is something in your soul, besides everything that you have told me, something very profound."

* * *

"There is no longer any doubt," he declares now to the sea breeze, "Dr. Ruiz is mistaken; he doesn't realize the extent of my love for Odete."

A long and loud whistle is heard; the ship sails. The young man, coming out of his reverie, looks longingly once again at the Lerin Islands, sees their lights fade and heads with determination towards his cabin.

* * *

It is ten o'clock in the morning when Torres goes ashore. Croma had made port in Genoa at daybreak. Odete does not go with him; her appointment to have her hair done for the farewell ball that evening keeps her on board.

The constant warnings over the loudspeaker can still be heard: "The ship will sail from Genoa at 12 noon. Please..."

He began to wander aimlessly through the streets and alleys in the vicinity of the docks, afraid of getting more than a few blocks away and not having enough time to get back to the ship. The area is typical of a waterfront: bars and restaurants create that mysterious climate inherent to a red light district.

Activity in the streets is essentially commercial. Italians gesticulate and argue in loud voices, perhaps over the price or quality of some merchandise, and sailors of many nationalities walk in pairs like curious tourists.

His attention isn't caught by anything in particular. He absorbs the atmosphere as though he had lived in it for a long time and has a vague sensation of having shared in some adventure in this place.

A small shop with trinkets displayed in the window reminds him of the souvenirs that he should take back to Brazil. He considers buying several things, but restrains himself. He'll take care of that in Rome, and, having made that decision, resumes walking slowly through the streets.

Suddenly, without realizing anybody is near him, he feels a touch on the arm: he turns and sees a poorly dressed woman with overdone make-up.

"Buy me a coffee, sweetheart, *per piacere?*"

Her bright red checked blouse and completely wrinkled skirt reveal their frequent wear. The wrinkled face and the puffy eyes reflect nights of debauchery and sleepless mornings.

The revulsion that he feels makes him jerk his arm away.

"*Per piacere,*" she begs submissively.

"I can't, I'm in *ritardo,*" he says in a grotesque mixture of Portuguese and Italian.

Having said that, he leaves in a hurry with broad strides and, reaching the corner, looks back and sees the woman still staring at him.

Rosa! he remembers suddenly. Eight years ago he had had the same feeling of revulsion. This event reveals the reason for his strange affinity to that environment.

Taken by surprise, he begins to walk slowly and, looking to each side, verifies that everything looks familiar and melancholy to him.

Forlorn and not knowing what to do or where to go, he enters a bar and orders coffee. Leaving a few minutes later and still gripped by that unexpected experience, he comes across a small church and, as though mysteriously drawn to it, enters.

* * *

The waiter serves them. Torres shows signs of strong emotion. Ruiz, perceiving that the young man wants to

175

unburden himself, pours wine into his glass and persuades him to take a long drink.

"I'm all ears," he says, after seeing the tranquilizing effect of the wine.

"What do you mean by that?"

"Come on, you know very well what I mean. What's the problem?"

"Do I look like I have one?"

"I've known you too long for you to try to fool me. Come on, let it out."

"Very well, you win."

Torres takes another sip of wine and begins to tell, with emotion, the events of that morning.

"... those similarities led me to go to church. I entered a little fearfully, like a thief in a police station. The place was silent; there was only a woman cleaning the side altars. The various statues decorating it revealed that it had a long tradition. Cautiously, almost on tiptoe, I went to the second pew, very close to the main altar. Upon the marble table there was a lace cloth which fell over the edges halfway to the floor. A red lamp burned to one side and everything was quiet. The tabernacle was facing me and I it. We continued to stare at each other a long time until I remembered something that had happened in my childhood. My first catechism teacher had taught me that the Spirit of Jesus Christ lived within it. I remembered this now in this Church. The tabernacle was closed, and I felt that God had closed himself off from me.

The face of the young man shows the tension of those moments.

I was desperate; I didn't want to be abandoned by Him. And, suddenly, without knowing why, I got up and began to

176

walk aimlessly about the church, anxiously trying in body and spirit to get away from that closed door. Minutes later I returned to the pew out of breath. My heart was pounding stronger and stronger to the point where it was trying to leap out of my chest. At the height of my anguish, when, for a moment, I thought I had lost my mind, I looked at the tabernacle and cried out, almost screaming, 'My God, help me for I know not what to do!' Having said that I became ecstatic, and I had the strange sensation that a tremor was rising from my feet to my head. My face was buried in my hands, and I cried as though the weeping was pouring out from my affliction."

Torres pauses and takes a deep breath.

"When I raised my head, I saw the sunlight reflected in colors on the wall and, somewhat caught up, I began to pray as though hypnotized. The faith of those prayers gave me a feeling of companionship with God and a feeling of well being came over me; it seemed like I was floating. I looked at the tabernacle and I felt that it had opened for me. Moments later, I noticed a crucifix above the altar and once again received the message: 'There is nothing beyond this.' I realized that everything that had been confused had been cleared up. Happiness overwhelmed me, and it was so great that I had the desire to shout out loud that I would never leave Him. At the height of this emotion, I said to Him: 'My God, I can no longer struggle against your forces; let Your will be done.' I closed my eyes and began slowly to utter some prayers; they were words that sprang forth calmly, causing my spirit to be freed from my body."

He pauses once again. The doctor remains silent, avoiding interrupting him. And he continues:

"I remained in that position for a long time, and when I came to my senses, I saw that more than an hour had gone by; Croma would be leaving shortly. I got up and began walking slowly and, as I passed by the icons of the saints, the pillars, pews and paintings, I felt as though I were part of them, as though my body was one of the bricks in the building. Near the door I made the sign of the cross and left. It was almost noon. Croma was blowing its whistle and I joyfully began to run."

He is quiet. His face betrays his emotions and a mystical peace puts a smile on his lips.

"I don't think I have to say which path I think I ought to follow, and I'm at peace with that. What surprises me, however, is how quickly I changed my mind. I feel that there's a kind of incongruity in all this," he says with awe. "Hours ago I was absolutely certain that I was going to marry Odete, and now I have definitely decided to follow my vocation."

"But that is perfectly normal. Some decisions, which seem to be made suddenly, are actually the result of a long and unconscious process of maturing."

"The approach to God," the doctor continues, "is something indefinable, but the means to and results of this process put faith to the test. I feel totally convinced that you have decided correctly. What concerns me now is Odete."

"I think I may have gone too far," he says, blaming himself.

"You acted honestly, so you have done nothing wrong. It was almost impossible, after so long an interval in the seminary, for you to measure your feelings towards Odete. The outcome has proven that they were signs of a transitory friendship."

"No," he interrupts abruptly, "I acted with complete sincerity; my commitment had taken on the character of

178

permanence and it could only be undone by a greater force, one which wound up influencing my choice."

"I stand corrected, then."

They stop talking, trying to think of something to say.

"The waiter is already looking at us threateningly. Let's leave before he starts to hover around us," proposes Ruiz.

They get up. The expression on Torres' face is one of peace.

Chapter X

"We can't put off the decision any longer about whether or not to go on with the voyage. Do you still insist on going back alone?" asks Odete.

The question surprises the young man, as he is unprepared to answer her and lacks the courage to tell her of his decision. His feelings for her and the reciprocity of that affection have turned this moment into a torment. They remain seated, slightly apart. Their hands, constantly held until recently, are now separated.

The deck at that hour is almost empty. The afternoon rest period and the preparations for the arrival the next day have kept most of the passengers in their cabins.

"Well..." he stammers without quite knowing what to say, "let's wait until tonight; by then I will have had time to consider it better."

"I can't wait any longer. I have to get my mother in the right frame of mind, and I have very little time to do it."

"Let's walk a little. This heat is stifling," he says, unbuttoning his collar.

"All right."

"I have to tell you something of the utmost importance," he states with decision, but then remains silent.

They begin to walk along the railing, still keeping apart and in silence. Arriving at the stern, they stop. Below, the propellers of the ship leave a long, foamy wake.

"I'm ready to listen to you."

"Listen to me?!"

"Yes, you said a little while ago that you had something of the utmost importance to say to me!"

"Oh, yes, I guess it can wait for later."

"No, it can't. You've changed a great deal overnight. What is it that is torturing you so?"

"But what leads you to that conclusion?" he exclaims, feigning surprise.

"Let's behave like intelligent people. Just looking at you I can see that there's been a sudden transformation."

He turns towards the sea and nervously breathes in the hot air of the Mediterranean. The movement of the propellers in the water makes an endless sound.

"Odete, I have become unaccustomed to using romantic words, but that won't stop me from saying that I have never been so much in love. These last few days have not only been extremely happy for me, but they have also marked my life forever," he confesses emotionally.

"Nevertheless, I...," he interrupts himself, "I don't know how to say..." he concludes in despair, unable to face her.

"Go on. I am not afraid," she encourages.

"Nevertheless, I have discovered that there exists something stronger than love between human beings. This stronger force has convinced me to continue with my religious vocation. I don't know how I can ask forgiveness..."

He turns toward Odete, expecting some criticism, and sees that she has lowered her head, trying to hide the tears flowing from her eyes.

"Forgive me," says Torres.

"You don't have to apologize," she says, deftly wiping away her tears, "after all, this isn't a complete surprise. Dr. Ruiz had already warned me about this."

"What? Dr. Ruiz? When?"

"He talked to me some days ago and told me that something very strong had induced you to mysticism, and his intention was to avert any harm that might come to me..." she stops, and, turning her face to one side, can no longer hold back more tears.

Torres is bewildered; his fingers drum on the railing nervously. He doesn't know what to say. Minutes later, she resumes talking.

"I'm sorry, I'm acting like a school girl," her reddened eyes try to force a smile. "There was some hope, and, small as it may have been, it was worth the risk," she explains, emotionally. "On Ste. Marguerite island I thought that my hopes were answered." She can't go on. She pulls away from him suddenly and goes over by the pool.

The young man goes after her.

"Don't say anything," she asks, "let me get used to the idea; everything is still confused and difficult for me."

They stop talking. A few middle aged couples who, unlike younger ones, take advantage of the day rather than the night, are strolling along, chattering. Odete and Torres look at them enviously. Their lives had already lost its romance and they were no longer capable of simple conversation between lovers.

"Can I ask something of you?"

"Of course."

"I want to meet you tonight."

"All right."

"See you later, then," she says in farewell, extending her hand to him and leaving as quickly as possible.

Torres gets up and goes to the chapel.

His love for Odete intermingles with the mystical feeling of his soul, and it is only with great effort that he manages to dominate the anguished desire to take her in his arms.

Chapter XI

"This has also been an unforgettable experience for me," says Ruiz to Torres over the last meal that they will have on board.

"For you?! But why?"

"For some time I've been nurturing a certain disbelief in the whole theory of psychoanalysis. It's not enough to reveal and eliminate the problems that cause mental illness. It may be true that talking about problems helps a lot, but if we don't lead the patient to see that this existence is useful, we can't offer a permanent cure. I can see now that truly vocational ecclesiastic life supplies the altruism and the suppression of material desires that are two of the main premises required for emotional stability."

"But it's necessary to include as well the existence of a supreme Being as an integral part of the whole," concludes the young man with conviction.

"I agree, and I think that this voyage, or perhaps age, I'm not sure which, will compel me to be more earnest in searching for God."

"That surprises me; I thought you were an agnostic!"

"This test forced me to remain neutral to both hypotheses; otherwise I might have influence you in your decision."

The silence is palpable.

"But as I was about to tell you..." continues the doctor, "I believed frustration to be the main reason for a man to enter the priesthood and, over the years, that fixed belief in the rules of the religious life would end up convincing him of the truth of his predestination. I later thought, and it was then that I made up the test, that, if a young seminarian such as yourself were given the opportunity to lead a normal life, the worldly pleasures would win out. But to my surprise, I discovered that I was wrong; throughout the entire test I was becoming desperate at seeing you on the threshold of taking a false step. You were at the cross roads of your affection for Odete and your mysticism."

They are interrupted by the waiter who serves them dessert, but shortly after the doctor resumes talking.

"If it weren't for the requirement, perhaps unnecessary, of priestly celibacy, you might be able to reconcile these paths, don't you think?"

"I disagree with you," the young man answers firmly. "There was a time when I thought so, but only now, despite everything, can I comprehend the wisdom of this requirement. It's very difficult to serve two masters; the burdens of matrimony are very heavy. Besides, the sacrifice of giving up marriage contributes to spiritual growth."

"If that's your belief, there is nothing more to discuss. Look, the waiter has already begun to hover about; we'd best leave."

Resignedly, they get up and head towards the door. In the corridor, the doctor stops and lights a cigarette.

"I'd like to take this opportunity to confess how grateful I am for having given me this experience," says Torres with emphasis. "The complete affirmation of my faith, which it has made possible, has given me a new look at life."

Chapter XII

At eight o'clock, as they had previously agreed, Torres and Odete meet at the main door on deck. They greet each other ceremoniously hoping to appear completely indifferent with their polished smiles. They go to the glass enclosed section, choose two chairs together, and sit down. The place is brightly lighted.

A meaningless conversation takes place since neither has the courage to bring up the subject that is eating away inside them. A little later, having exhausted all the possible subjects, they lapse into a long silence. It's up to Odete to broach the subject.

"I think there's no point in avoiding the matter that brought us here," her expression becomes serious and her face is drawn with all the unhappiness that she feels. "This afternoon I asked for this meeting because at that time I just couldn't speak," she states with emotion and not facing him. "I thought that these few hours would be enough for me to calm down, but I confess that I was mistaken."

"It's the same thing with me," he declares, upset. "There were times when I began to doubt the correctness of my decision. I don't know if I was sufficiently clear with you; the force that attracts me to God is so strong that it has become uncontrollable."

186

"You don't have to justify yourself; Dr. Ruiz has made me understand your reasons. What I want to tell you is that I don't hold any resentment towards you."

"Thank you, I..."

"Wait, let me finish..."

Torres consents with a nod of his head and she continues:

"It's a great consolation to me that we have broken off so that you could follow your vocation."

Another silence ensues. Feeling the impending definitive separation, Torres begins to despair upon understanding that he has lost Odete forever, and he recognizes, beyond the shadow of a doubt, how great is his love for her.

"I want to confess something to you as well. I will never forget you, and I tell you in all sincerity that under different circumstances I would marry you without hesitation."

"You can't imagine how happy that makes me," says Odete in a husky voice. "I will never forget you, either. Now, if you'll permit me, I would like to say goodbye. I had so much to say to you, but I can't seem to talk anymore..."

They get up and look profoundly at each other.

"Well, we began as friends, and we end as friends," says the girl, holding out her hand. Her tearful, shining eyes join a smile that momentarily softens her face.

"We end as friends," he repeats.

"Goodbye, then!" she says, withdrawing her hand and leaving quickly.

"Goodbye!" responds Torres in a whisper.

Upon awakening the next day, Croma is already anchored in Naples. The loudspeaker issues orders every few minutes, but the deafening babble makes them difficult to understand: stewards rush here and there. Everyone on the ship is all excited; baggage is piled up in the corridors impeding traffic; the confusion is as complete as possible.

The passengers, handing over their baggage, head toward the exits of the ship and line up on the two gangplanks that will take them back to land.

Torres awaits Ruiz at the foot of one of the gangplanks. They had agreed to share a taxi into town, but some problem has detained the doctor on board. The young man's impatience increases with the constant succession of happy passengers that go by him. As his uneasiness reaches its height, to his surprise he comes face to face with Odete and her mother as they descend the last few steps.

Upon seeing him, the girl hesitates and almost stops. Their serious looks cross, and, in a quick glance, she notices the impeccable clerical suit of the young man.

They smile. Averting his eyes and already some distance away, she can still see in her mind the stiffness of the collar worn by Torres.

"If that boy really liked you so much, why did he leave you?" asks the mother a few minutes later.

"Mother, it's difficult to answer the 'whys' of spiritual things."

"Well, you can't say I didn't warn you," she replies, unsatisfied. "He ended up fooling you the whole time."

"You can rest assured as far as that is concerned; after all, I was the one who was wrong by trying to make him give up his vocation."

A seagull glides over the water slightly above the ship. Its flight is sustained by a slight movement of the wings. The head hung low sweeps the marine depths.

He who wishes to serve God must renounce everything without hope of reward. An inner peace, however, will show on his face a smile of joy which has no equal here on earth.

188

Regis Castro Regis

Rabboni and **Jesus Loves You** are books of prayer and meditation, based on the Word of God. They address themes that lead you to greater peace, joy, love, physical and spiritual healing, pardon, blessing, salvation, faith in Jesus, and the fullness of life.

Regis Castro & Maïsa Castro

Jesus Visits You (Rachel) was written for you, woman, who loves, cares, works and suffers for your happiness and that of your family. God is now giving you the opportunity of salvation; which may never happen again like this.

Regis Castro & Maïsa Castro

Healing through Blessing (Blessing upon Blessing)
In this book you will learn to take possession of the Word of God. You will also learn the prayer of faith that moves the hand of God.

Regis Castro & Maïsa Castro

Raïssa is a very emotional book, not only because of its subject, but for the poetry contained in its lines. The spirit of the characters is projected in such a way that it is impossible not to be touched by them.

Regis Castro Regis

Rosary of Liberation is based on the Word of God and should be prayed with faith for the glory of the powerful name of Jesus Christ and to seek healing, salvation, and liberation.
Regis Castro & Maïsa Castro

Persevere in the Love of God shows the way for this and the blessings that God pours in the lives of those who, with all confidence and loyalty, persevere in Him.

Book of the Family — healing and salvation for you and your family presents some of the powerful weapons to be used against the spiritual forces of evil which destroy your life and that of your family.
Regis Castro & Maïsa Castro

Eternal Love presents the solution that God offers for all our problems of courtship, marriage and family.
Regis Castro & Maïsa Castro

Jesus Is My Friend was written precisely so that you may know more about the power of healing, salvation and liberation which are embodied in the name of Jesus and His Word.
Regis Castro & Maïsa Castro

Jesus Wants to Heal Your Life was inspired in talks about the Word of God given by the authors throughout their ministry of evangelization in radio programs, prayer groups, encounters, spiritual retreats, etc.
Regis Castro & Maïsa Castro

The Powerful Hand of Jesus in My Heart
The first chapter of this book may help you to open up to Jesus Christ and resolutely verify the love of God for you. The rest of the chapters also have, as their objective, the communication of a personal experience to you of the transforming power of God in your life.
Regis Castro & Maïsa Castro

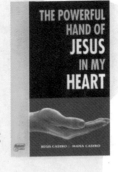

The Endearing Hands of Mary
This book is written for persons who have fallen and want to rise again, by the grace and mercy of God, through Jesus Christ and His Mother, Mary.
Regis Castro Regis

Ping-Pong Praise
This praise, besides its principal effect which is to exalt our God, teaches everyone, from the little child to the old man, to praise Him from the heart, with simplicity and for all things, thus fulfilling His word.
Regis Castro & Maïsa Castro

Prayers of Power collects a serie of prayers, ranging from the day–to–day ones that are part of the Word of God and the tradition of the church to those spontaneously used in charismatic prayer groups.

Prayer of Power II is another volume of prayers. Like the others, it is intended to lead readers to an ever more profound personal experience of the merciful love of God through prayer.

God's Promises to You

You wih find *God's Promises to You* in the Holy Scriptures which indicate the solution, through the power of the Holy Spirit, for all your personal, family and professional problems. Consult the Bible daily, read it, meditate on it praying and obtaining, though faith, what God's promises have for your every need.

Learn how to bring into your life the tranforming power of the Word of God.

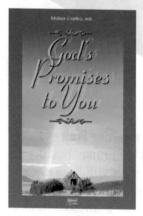

Maïsa Castro

Pray for Us, O Holy Mother of God!

With joy and in thanksgiving to God, we place in your hands the book Pray for Us, O Holy Mother of God! In it, you will find prayers, rosaries, novenas and especific devotions to Our Lady which will bear great fruit for your spiritual life. This book will also arouse in you a special love of the Virgin Mary and a sincere and trusting devotion to her power of intercession with Jesus.

God's Advice for You

The Book of Proverbs is rich in wisdom. It was necessary to divide and separate its messages into chapters that contain themes for spiritual, family, social and professional life.
Regis Castro, ed.

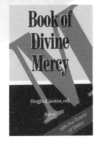  

Regis Castro, ed.   Raïssa Castro Oliveira, ed.

Book of Divine Mercy, Book of Forgiveness and **Book of Joyfulness** are books of prayer. They should be read slowly by you – in prayer – meditating well on the meaning of each verse and assimilating its content through faith. Thus, the Word of God, gathered into your heart, is experienced through the action of the divine Holy Spirit and will bear fruit in your life.